# JONATHAN LETHEM

Wo...

Berlin Prize

MacArthur Foundation "Genius" grant

National Book Critics Circle Award

Macallan Gold Dagger

Locus Award

Crawford Award

# The Collapsing Frontier

*plus*

## PM PRESS OUTSPOKEN AUTHORS SERIES

1. *The Left Left Behind*
   Terry Bisson

2. *The Lucky Strike*
   Kim Stanley Robinson

3. *The Underbelly*
   Gary Phillips

4. *Mammoths of the Great Plains*
   Eleanor Arnason

5. *Modem Times 2.0*
   Michael Moorcock

6. *The Wild Girls*
   Ursula K. Le Guin

7. *Surfing the Gnarl*
   Rudy Rucker

8. *The Great Big Beautiful Tomorrow*
   Cory Doctorow

9. *Report from Planet Midnight*
   Nalo Hopkinson

10. *The Human Front*
    Ken MacLeod

11. *New Taboos*
    John Shirley

12. *The Science of Herself*
    Karen Joy Fowler

13. *Raising Hell*
    Norman Spinrad

14. *Patty Hearst & The Twinkie Murders: A Tale of Two Trials*
    Paul Krassner

15. *My Life, My Body*
    Marge Piercy

16. *Gypsy*
    Carter Scholz

17. *Miracles Ain't What They Used to Be*
    Joe R. Lansdale

**18.** *Fire.*
Elizabeth Hand

**19.** *Totalitopia*
John Crowley

**20.** *The Atheist in the Attic*
Samuel R. Delany

**21.** *Thoreau's Microscope*
Michael Blumlein

**22.** *The Beatrix Gates*
Rachel Pollack

**23.** *A City Made of Words*
Paul Park

**24.** *Talk like a Man*
Nisi Shawl

**25.** *Big Girl*
Meg Elison

**26.** *The Planetbreaker's Son*
Nick Mamatas

**27.** *The First Law of Thermodynamics*
James Patrick Kelly

**28.** *Utopias of the Third Kind*
Vandana Singh

**29.** *Night Shift*
Eileen Gunn

**30.** *The Collapsing Frontier*
Jonathan Lethem

**31.** *The Presidential Papers*
John Kessel

**32.** *The Last Coward on Earth*
Cara Hoffman

# The Collapsing Frontier

*plus*

Calvino's "Lightness" and the Feral Child of History

*plus*

In Mugwump Four

*and much more*

## Jonathan Lethem

PM PRESS | 2024

"David Bowman and the Furry-Girl School of American Fiction" first
    appeared in the *New Yorker*, January 2, 2019.
"Snowden in the Labyrinth" first appeared in the *New York Review of Books*,
    October 24, 2019.
"My Year of Reading Lemmishly" first appeared in the *London Review of
    Books*, February 10, 2022.
"The Collapsing Frontier" first appeared under the title "Narrowing Valley" in
    the *New Yorker*, October 31, 2022.
The above pieces have been lightly edited for this collection.
"Calvino's 'Lightness' and the Feral Child of History" and "In Mugwump
    Four" are original to this volume.

ISBN (paperback): 978-1-62963-488-3
ISBN (ebook): 978-1-62963-654-2
ISBN (hardcover): 979-8-88744-029-3
LCCN: 2022942533

Series editor: Terry Bisson
Cover design by John Yates/www.stealworks.com
Author photo by Ian Byers-Gambler
Insides by Jonathan Rowland

10 9 8 7 6 5 4 3 2 1

Printed in the USA

# Contents

David Bowman and the Furry-Girl School of
American Fiction                                           1

Snowden in the Labyrinth                                   25

The Collapsing Frontier                                    53

"Rooms Full of Old Books Are Immortal Enough              65
for Me"
Jonathan Lethem interviewed by Terry Bisson

My Year of Reading Lemmishly                               77

Calvino's "Lightness" and the Feral Child of History     113

In Mugwump Four                                           137

Secret Bibliography                                       157

About the Author                                          159 for Michael Kandel

# David Bowman and the Furry-Girl School of American Fiction

Introduction to David Bowman's *Big Bang* (Little, Brown, 2019)

## 1. They Also Wrote

FOR YEARS I THOUGHT I'd begin an essay with the title "They Also Wrote." This wasn't a plan, exactly, but a notion, barely more than a title. The idea was to write a kind of general manifesto on behalf of forgotten authors. I'd likely never have done it. By a certain point I'd made my eccentric preference for out-of-print and neglected fiction, for the noncanonical dark horses—Flann O'Brien over James Joyce, say—abundantly clear (probably irritatingly so, for any reader who was paying attention). With the help of the New York Review Books imprint and a few other heroic publishing programs, I'd been involved, a few times, in dragging a few of my pets back into view—Bernard Wolfe, Anna Kavan, Don Carpenter. Other times I'd simply been delighted to see it done, as if according to my whims, but without lifting a finger.

We may be living, in fact, in the great age of "rediscovered" authors. Younger readers want to talk to me, all the time, about Shirley Jackson and John Williams and, of course, Philip K. Dick, who's become so renowned that very few people remember that at the time of his death he was largely forgotten, and out of print.

Perhaps at a time when canons have fragmented and been assaulted, and working authors seem compromised by social-media overfamiliarity and three-and-a-half-star verdicts, these honorably silent dark horses are the best repository for our old sacred feeling, the one cultivated in the semiprivacy between a reader and a favorite book. Living writers, now that we've gotten such a close look at them, are pretty embarrassing. Famous authors of the past? Mostly blowhards. Posthumously celebrated writers, on the other hand, all seem to walk under the grace of Kafka's umbrella, with Melville and Emily Dickinson.

Plenty of remarkable books still slip through the rediscovery net. I wouldn't have put money on David Bowman's chances. Certainly, I'd never have imagined that my largely forgotten old friend, author of two slim out-of-print novels and one out-of-print book of music journalism, would be reincarnated in the form of an epic novel about celebrity and power in the postwar twentieth century, one he didn't finish soon enough to submit to publishers before he died. Sure, I'd known *Big Bang*—which Bowman also sometimes liked to call *Tall Cool One*—existed. He'd shown me portions of it over the years. I'm probably not the only person who saw pages. But the notion that he'd reached a satisfying conclusion to what seemed his most Quixotic writing journey, let alone that anyone would ever usher it into print—this never seemed remotely likely.

No, if Bowman were heard from again, I'd assumed it would be because some dedicated publisher had chosen to reprint his first novel, from 1992, *Let the Dog Drive*. It was his only success, really, among the three books published during his lifetime, despite being published by NYU Press and therefore receiving barely anything in the way of a publicity campaign. (The early '90s were an unmatched era in the history of publicity campaigns for novels; it was Bowman who joked to me that when he witnessed Donna Tartt's rollout in *Vanity Fair* he thought, "Wow, I wish *I* had a novel out," and then, "Wait a minute, I do have a novel out!") *Let the Dog Drive*, an antic noir comedy about dysfunctional family, interspersed literary and pop-cultural references with arresting sex and violence. It gained rave reviews in both the *Times Book Review* and the *New Yorker*, despite featuring nothing more in the way of jacket blurbs than an excerpt from a letter to Bowman from Joan Didion, thanking him for mentioning her in the novel. (That he'd written to Didion was, I'd learn, typical of Bowman's ingenuous approach to celebrities, literary and otherwise, who fascinated him; more on this soon).

During Bowman's 1995 book tour for the Penguin paperback of *Let the Dog Drive*, in 1995, he visited the Diesel bookstore, in Oakland. I was one of a handful who attended. I asked him to autograph my copy of the NYU hardcover, and gave him a copy of my then-fresh first novel, *Gun, with Occasional Music*. Bowman inscribed my copy, "To Jonathan—six figures in your future!" Bowman candidly dreamed of glory for both of us, from the inception of our friendship. Yet it was our dual marginality that created the bond.

## 2. The Bowman Tapes

Bowman returned to New York, and I stayed, for the moment, in my garret in Berkeley. Almost immediately, we'd talk on the phone nearly every day. Bowman was my first conduit to the contemporary literary New York City of the late '90s, which I was now working my courage up to enter, and which was almost wholly mysterious to me; growing up in Brooklyn hadn't constituted any form of preliminary encounter. Bowman was marvelously charismatic on the phone. His tone amused and conspiratorial, he began every call *in medias res*, with the word "so . . ." Then he'd leap in midstream, resuming some trailing thought from an earlier conversation, even if it was only one he'd been having with himself.

Yet the phone wasn't enough. Bowman besieged me with charmingly nutty handwritten letters, many of them containing scissor-and-gluepot collages, usually incorporating elements from the New York tabloids—Page Six squibs concerning the kind of writers who generated Page Six squibs: Mailer, McInerney, his beloved Didion, or downtown figures who'd risen to stardom, like Patti Smith, Jim Jarmusch, David Byrne—combined with Bowman's own cartoonish Sharpie scribbles or his personal erotic photography. He'd call these cut-ups "charms"—they were meant to convey writerly luck. One I still have tacked up over my desk was called the "Dancing DeLillos Charm": a row of Rockettes with Don DeLillo's head atop each dancer.

Yet there's more: the Bowman Tapes. He and his wife regularly rented a cabin in Montauk, and while there he'd pace the beach, drinking beer and monologuing to me into a tape recorder. The cassettes arrived in the mail, incoherently labelled. I'd pop them into my car or home tape player and listen. They were hypnotic, outlandish, and boring at once. Bowman's monologues were elaborately themed—usually some variation on his obsession with writerly ambition, and how it was cursed for him, for me, and nearly anybody, by the afflictions of personal fate. He'd inaugurate each rant with certain key phrases to which he'd return, as if in song. Bowman was a master at a kind of verbal plate-spinning routine, but he was also a helpless digressionist, and sometimes a plate on the far side of the stage would be forgotten for twenty minutes or more. Sometimes you'd have to flip the tape over to find out whether he'd forgotten his theme.

This is improbable, but much about Bowman is improbable: he sent more tapes than I found time to listen to. I recall my girlfriend complaining about how they'd begun filling up the floor space in the passenger side of my Toyota Corolla. I did my best to keep up, but it was hopeless. On the tapes, Bowman's dreams and schemes were interspersed with the crunch of his feet on the wet Montauk beach at night, and though I haven't listened to one of the Bowman tapes in nearly two decades, I can still hear that gravel crunch and the heavy breathing of his pauses for thought, as if it recurs in my nightly dreams.

### 3. The Lot 49 Method

Bowman's loyalty and generosity were simply immense, in those first years, while I remained stranded in Berkeley, far from the action, and our friendship was conducted by phone, tape, and charm. After three books, I'd been orphaned at Harcourt Brace, and needed a new publisher, but I was a pretty small fish. My agent had an offer from Doubleday, but Bowman, working behind the scenes, turned it into a small auction with his own publisher, Little, Brown. (I landed at Doubleday.) The book in question needed a new title, the first task I needed to perform for my shiny new publisher, and I was flailing. Bowman walked me through it: use the Lot 49 Method, he told me. I had to ask what he meant. "'The crying of lot 49' is the last line of *The Crying of Lot 49*," he explained. "What's the last line of your book?" I looked: my last line included a phrase similar to "as she climbed across the table." That same book was blurbless. Bowman, acting on his own, forced it on, of all people, Jim Harrison. Likely bewildered but charmed, as people tended to be on early encounter with Bowman's manic style, Harrison improbably gave forth with a blurb. I doubt my new publisher had any idea how that happened—I barely understood it myself—but they probably assumed Harrison had been my teacher somewhere, or been a friend of my dad's.

### 4. The Furry-Girl School

At some point early on Bowman coined a name for us: The Furry-Girl School of American Fiction. He'd named it after a character in my second novel, *Amnesia Moon*—a girl, specifically, who was furry. I don't mean "furry" in the modern polymorphous-perverse sense of a fetish for dressing up in costumes and having sex; I mean that her body was covered in light fur. To Bowman, the character was emblem of what he and I loved most in the books we loved: not "heart," exactly, but some eccentric and character or motif, a tic or inside joke, almost, one that made the book *personal* to the author and in turn to the reader who loved it. A book could be impressive without containing this quality, which was quickly shortened to "Furry." In Bowman's reasoning—always composed of instantaneous certainties—almighty DeLillo, for instance, had written books both Furry (*End Zone*, *White Noise*) and not (*Players*, *Underworld*). Mailer had never been Furry in his life. Chandler was Furry, Ellroy not. And so on. Swept up, anointed, I consented even when it made no sense, and we indexed the whole world on the Furry Scale.

The Furry-Girl School needed a female member—this was my suggestion, and I nominated a writer named Cathryn Alpert, who'd written a funny, Furry, and in some ways Bowmanesque novel called *Rocket City*. From the clues (small-press publication in hardcover, for one thing) Alpert was as much outsider, as much dark-horse, as Bowman and I felt ourselves to be. We called or e-mailed, out of the blue; or possibly I turned up at a reading and announced us to her. Bowman's charms worked at a distance (perhaps they worked best at a distance) and Cathryn Alpert, who'd heard of neither of us before this, quickly consented. The Furry-Girl School had three members now.

## 5. Chloe and Snoot

David Bowman would turn out to one of the most isolated people I've ever known—isolated on the profoundest levels by a certain traumatic displacement from ordinary human consolation. Yet on a day-to-day basis he wasn't strictly *alone*. Bowman had a wife. Chloe Wing was older than Bowman and seemed almost infinitely kind and patient with him, if sometimes also rather distant, impassive (later, I'd view this as a survival trait on Chloe's part). He also had a dog, the beloved Snoot, a tall black-and-white hound with sensitive paws. Snoot suffered: he endured treatments to his paws, and for digestive troubles and other ailments. Bowman, helpless in his devotion, suffered with the dog.

When I moved back to New York City and first visited Bowman and Chloe and Snoot in their beautiful Manhattan apartment, his life seemed enviable. From the distance of California my new friend had appeared to know so many editors and writers. I was now ready to be swept up in his world, to begin our friendship in person, rather than long-distance. In fact, up close, my great friend was quickly exposed as a person whose stark limitations, whose damage, were the equal of his charisma and brilliance. Almost overnight, I began at some level to take care of Bowman, instead of the reverse.

### 6. Dogboy and Sarge

If David Bowman was such a dear friend, why do I keep calling him Bowman? Well, I never called him David. To others, I called him Bowman, as he'd called me Lethem, to others. It was Bowman's habit always and only to last-name writers (Didion, Lish, Moody, et al.) Then he'd adopt hard-and-fast nicknames for interpersonal address. At his suggestion, I called him Dogboy, and he called me, at first, Amnesia Boy, after my second novel, *Amnesia*

*Moon.* Pretty soon he switched me to Sarge, which was how he addressed me for the rest of his life. Bowman called me Sarge because, he explained, he always followed my commands, as if in a war movie, as if we were going over a hill.

The "commands" in question? I'd tell Bowman *not* to do things. After I'd moved to New York, I'd begun to realize how he was serially alienating the magazine editors upon whom he depended, as well his book publicists and other editorial subordinates. He freaked people out with his bizarre pitches, his strange, insinuating late-night calls and emails, his impetuous rages over poorly specified minor betrayals. He knew many writers and editors, yes, but now I saw that nearly all of them had learned, or were learning, or would soon learn, to treat him with kid gloves. There came a point when I understood I'd never met anyone who devoted as large a share of his (vast) creative energy to impulses that were sheerly disastrous, that he had to be talked out of.

To my shame (on behalf of Bowman), most of the victims of his tirades were women. He'd seethe endlessly about men who'd crossed him—like the businessman who'd once kicked at Snoot on Second Avenue—but it was only against women that Bowman truly uncorked his rage. To my shame (on my own behalf), my interventions weren't so much with his victims in mind as they were intended to save Bowman from himself.

## 7. Loves

Bowman loved beer and traveled to a special warehouse in Brooklyn to purchase the exotic imported bottles he craved. This was nearly the only thing that could get him onto the subway—he otherwise preferred to walk Snoot on the Lower East Side, or to stay at home.

Bowman loved Bob Dylan, inordinately, and collected Dylan bootlegs, but to my astonishment had never been to see Dylan play live. Bowman loved Patti Smith, inordinately. He loved her earliest music, raging and foul-mouthed, and he seemed always to be searching for an equivalent in his curiosity about PJ Harvey, Thea Gilmore, and so forth. He loved Marianne Faithfull, too; fair to say he was electrified by foul-mouthed women in general. He loved Lou Reed, Gillian Welch, Thomas Carlyle, Elizabeth McCracken's *The Giant's House*, Cormac McCarthy's *Blood Meridian*, Dr. Seuss, and dogs.

Bowman loved New York City. He'd come from elsewhere—Wisconsin, then Vermont—but embraced the city without looking back. The city's greatest exponents seem to latch on to it as Balzac's Lucien Chardon latches on to Paris, in *Lost Illusions*, after arriving from the provinces: Dawn Powell, Andy Warhol, et al.

Bowman loved film noir, but I don't recall him caring particularly for film otherwise. I don't recall any affection for soul music, or science fiction, or food in general. He lived a few blocks from Veselka but declined ever to meet me there for the late-night plates of pierogis that reminded me so much of my teenage years—frequenting Veselka again had been one of the several things I was sure I'd moved back to New York City to do.

## 8. The Truck

On Montauk, in 1989, Bowman had been walking alone on a road when was hit and nearly killed by a truck (his *Times* obituary reads "car," but he always called it a truck when we spoke). He suffered major head trauma and was in a coma for a month, during which he was ministered by his wife Chloe, to whom he said he owed his life. *Let the Dog Drive* was largely finished, before the accident, but when he awoke from his coma he wasn't aware he'd written a book, and had to read the draft dozens of times before he understood that it was up to him to finish it. His friend, Eric Schneider, to whom it is dedicated, told his obituarist, Paul Vitello, that the book "helped him remember who he was."

This may be true. It surely is, in part. But it is also the case that the last portions of *Let the Dog Drive* portray scenes of torture and revenge which plunge the book into a darkness for which the earlier two-thirds have scantly prepared a reader to endure. I didn't have Chloe's or Eric Schneider's luck, of knowing Bowman both before and after the accident. I do know that one of Bowman's alternate nicknames for himself was Vengeance Boy—and that as long as I knew him he saw himself as wronged by the universe. I know that he saw himself as a person who suffered, on a daily basis, and sought alleviation in beer, rock and roll, and fantasies of righteous justice being inflicted on his many persecutors. He could offer humorous perspective on his condition, but it wasn't something over which he appeared to have any control.

David Bowman died, in 2012, of a massive brain hemorrhage. I'd moved back to California just a year before, and I learned of his death from Chloe, who reached me by telephone. I was stunned. Bowman and I had been out of touch for a year or more, and the news I feared was the reverse: I knew that Chloe was mortally sick with cancer, and that Bowman might at some point tell me that he had been left even more alone in the world. (Chloe did follow, a year later.)

"He walked into our bedroom and told me he had a terrible headache," Chloe told me, and explained that he then fell to the floor and was dead within minutes. "It was a good death," she added, whether to console me or herself or because she felt it was so, I don't know. It seemed to me a parenthesis had closed, as though the truck had come to claim him. How strange to consider that the years between the injury and his death, the twenty-three years in which he published three books and wrote at least two more, the years in which I'd known him, could be seen as merely a kind of dispensation.

The question I can't avoid: How much was Vengeance Boy a product of brain trauma?

### 9. Just Like Tom Thumb's Blues

In the first flush of my return to New York, in the period when I projected Bowman as one of my great life's companions, without qualification, and before I'd understood how difficult it was for him to be out of his self-soothing routines, his Snoot walks, and away from his desk and telephone, I dragged him to a Bob Dylan concert. I saw this as my duty. I was seeing Dylan live a lot in that period.

The concert was in New Jersey, at the Performing Arts Center, in Newark. I was riding there with my friend Michael, and others, and I arranged to pick Bowman up at his doorstep. This was a great calamitous carload of fools wreathed in pot smoke, and in retrospect I'm amazed that I lured Bowman into the back seat. He had a wide-eyed, daft look that said he was amazed himself to have been lured. He wore a long trench coat, buttoned to the neck. "I just hope he plays 'Tom Thumb's Blues,'" Bowman said, and I warned him not to expect it: Dylan rarely plays that song, and never plays what you most wish to hear. Of course, we arrived late to the concert, in a crazy fever to park and go inside. We'd calculated our trip to miss the opening act, a regular sport for Michael and me when Dylangoing, so Dylan was already playing.

At the routine frisk inside the turnstiles, a security guard made Bowman open his trench coat. Immediately visible were two beers, Bowman's beloved imported bottles, one in each of his flannel shirt's pockets. Bowman gave a sheepish shrugging smile, one I'll never forget. The guard, shaking his head, confiscated the bottles. We rushed up to the highest level of the auditorium to find our seats in the dark. As we sat, Bowman frisked himself this time, reproducing the sheepish smile. He revealed a bottle that had survived the guard's inspection. Then another, and another—he still possessed *three* bottles, which had been secreted who-knows-where, in his sleeves or in the trench coat's interior pockets. As we took our seats, gazing down on Dylan and his band's heads from the upper deck, Dylan finished one song and began another: "Just Like Tom Thumb's Blues."

## 10. Bunny Has a Hairball

*Let the Dog Drive* gave Bowman his chance to move to a major publisher. He followed his eccentric book with an even more eccentric one, called *Bunny Modern*, set in a future where electricity has vanished, and armed nannies protect a diminishing pool of babies from kidnappers while cranked-up on a drug called Vengeance. Around the time I moved back to New York Bowman was revising the pages obsessively; his expectations for the book were immense. When he finally showed it to me he delivered it in what he called the Bunny Box—a kind of three-dimensional collage object, much larger than it needed to be to contain what was a very brief manuscript. His impatience for me to read it, and sanctify it as "Furry," was formidable.

There came a strange misadventure. This was before cell phones. I'd read the book overnight, and Bowman had stood by for my assessment, but I had an urgent appointment and had to leave word with my friend Maureen, knowing he'd call. The phrase I asked Maureen to pass along was, "The Bunny is furry." Maureen, panicked by Bowman's urgency, blurted out, "The Bunny has a hairball." Bowman exploded. She apologized, but it was too late. An hour or two later, when I was able to reach him directly, his only words for me were "The Bunny has a hairball? The Bunny has a *hairball?*" He'd sat stewing, drinking beer, and trying to interpret Maureen's colorful slip. The only interpretations he could on were dire ones. I worked to calm him down.

Maureen might have been prescient. There were US writers who'd lately preceded Bowman in offering dystopian fantasias under the cover of traditional literary publishing: Steve Erickson, Katherine Dunn, Paul Auster. Kirstin Bakis's *Lives of the Monster Dogs* had found a nice success in New York, the year before. Bowman was envious—dogs were his thing—but also believed it auspicious for his book. Yet he was at least ten years ahead of the great fashion for dystopias in highbrow circles, and anyhow, hadn't judged how his book's slightness, and its vein of real perversity, might play against it.

Bowman been a dark-horse success with *Let the Dog Drive*, but now he'd lost a major publisher some money, and, worse, exhausted their good faith with his badgering calls and office visits. The book's failure wasn't another truck, perhaps, but it sliced off another layer of Bowman's droll, perversely jubilant outlook, and deepened his sense of being misused by fate, perhaps even being conspired against—by whom, exactly, he wouldn't have been able to say.

## 11. Shit on Your Shoes

Yet Bowman was never self-pitying. Were I tempted to wallow or complain, at some disappointment inflicted on my own aspirations—the fact that *As She Climbed across the Table* had gone completely unreviewed in the *New York Times*, say, leaving me, despite my new publisher's exertions, still a cult quantity—Bowman would offer a kind of noncommiseration commiseration. He'd invoke a favorite term: "Sarge," he'd say, "you've got shit on your shoes." I wish I could reproduce for you the tone of affectionate philosophical mordancy with which he'd pronounce it. (In fact, it's surely on the tapes, a dozen times over.)

By "shit on your shoes" Bowman meant, in my case, that I'd had my early stories published in science-fiction magazines, and attended science-fiction conventions, and traded blurbs with science-fiction writers, and not concealed or apologized for those facts. In his own case, he meant his publication with NYU Press—and in both our cases, the fact that (unlike Kirsten Bakis) we'd come in the door with no MFA program or Ivy League pedigree. We'd simply walked in with shit on our shoes, such that those with a nose aversive to the kinds of shit we bore would reliably shun us. In fact, this isn't too lousy a diagnosis of an awful lot of literary fate-casting: that the first impression, or size of the first advance, was predeterminative in any but the luckiest or most tenacious of cases. For Bowman this was something to sigh over, to open a bottle of beer over. And then he'd resume work.

## 12. Bowman Also Wrote

The brevity of his two published novels notwithstanding, Bowman was a workaholic, and as voluminous on the page as on the tapes. Because his brain injury had made his eyesight difficult, and made him prone to headaches, he edited his pages at a giant font size, sixteen- or eighteen-point, as I remember it. (He blew his font up to an even more enormous size for public readings, I learned, when we gave one together at KGB, the two of us along with Amanda Filipacchi playing to an absolutely packed room for what was only my second-ever reading in New York City—a thrilling event for me.) In the years following *Bunny Modern* he worked on three fiction projects concurrently: *Big Bang* (or *Tall*

*Cool One*); another novel in the phantasmagorical vein of *Bunny Modern*, called *Women on the Moon*; and a novella based on a conflation of Theodore Kaczynski's anti-technological manifesto and Kafka's *Letter to His Father*, called either *The Unabomber's Letter to His Father* or, confusingly, *A Letter to His Unabomber*. Also confusingly, Bowman sent me portions of all three manuscripts, but never an entirety (perhaps superstitious of another hairball-assessment), or even a first chapter. Even more confusingly, his spelling in first draft work was always and persistently terrible, either because of some kind of dyslexia or because of his brain injury, I wasn't sure.

So much about Bowman was increasingly confusing and dismaying to me—had he really telephoned X or Y and said aloud what he'd *told* me he'd said aloud to them? Why would anyone do these things? I'd run into writers Bowman had introduced me to, initially, and when his name came up, they'd shake their heads, and describe some kind of breach or ultimatum or farcical misconstruction that had come between them. I'd like to say I defended him, or apologized for him—there were times when I did. But Sarge couldn't work miracles, couldn't preempt every crisis, couldn't work in retrospect, or erase words he'd spoken aloud.

Gradually, to my shame, this sense that Bowman was making himself personally indefensible crept in and poisoned my belief in his writing. He was still one of my favorite writers, just as he was still my friend. But the non-long-term viability of his persona, of his personal approach, began to seem to me analogous to the notion that very many people weren't likely to agree with me about his writing. Besides, his fiction wasn't going into print, where I could advocate for it. It was piling up in his house, and in the e-mail excerpts, which he'd fling my way, increasingly, confusingly, at random intervals, without clarifying the purpose to which he'd shared the particular sequence he'd shared. The e-mails appeared to be like the tapes, meant for me alone, even if they contained many brilliant, singular passages—lines I'd quote, or be thrilled to have written myself. The whole problem of Bowman was becoming something like the oversupply of tapes on the passenger-side floor of my old Toyota Corolla.

Nevertheless, I encouraged each project in turn. The Unabomber letter seemed especially promising to me, not merely for its clever hook and newsy relevance. I knew that Bowman was enraged at his parents. He hadn't spoken to anyone from his immediate family for over fifteen years, he claimed. I felt this unprocessed rage impeded his art, and his life. So, the reference to Kafka's famous outpouring seemed to suggest Bowman might use the project as a vehicle to confront all that went unconfronted. But no. In the pages he sent, the emphasis, bizarrely, was on *literary* injustices, on outrages within the publishing world of contemporary New York—it read like a Bowman tape, transcribed. I demoted the project in my regard and encouraged him to work on *Women on the Moon* instead. It had that wonderful title, and seemed to capture some of his daffy reverence for Chloe, for all women. The mammoth project, the one about the Kennedys, Lou Reed, Howard Hunt, J.D. Salinger, Elvis, the one about everything and anything that he'd ever known or read or intuited about the postwar American backdrop against which we'd both come of age, all of which haunted his work implicitly, haunted every line, but was here being treated *explicitly*—that couldn't possibly work. Could it?

I didn't think Bowman could carry it off. It seemed like something Norman Mailer would try for, and something Mailer would fail at. Possibly Bowman had miscast himself, as Mailer or DeLillo or Doctorow, a white-elephant novelist, when he really ought to stick to his Richard Brautigan dreams, his termite operations. This was also a matter of publishing pragmatics—who, after Bunny Modern, was going to sign on the dotted line for a thousand Bowman pages? Most simply, I couldn't imagine he'd finish it.

I should have known better.

## 13. The Fall of the Furry-Girl School

The fall of the Furry-Girl School of American Fiction took the form, on one side, of abrupt tragic farce, and on the other side of slow degradation, and my long shame. The tragic farce was this: Cathryn Alpert and her husband had never met Bowman, and were coming to New York on other business and had planned a rendezvous. As I recall it, they were staying in a Midtown hotel. Time was tight. Some plan was in place—surely it had been difficult, for Bowman, to make such a plan, since meeting people, new people, at an appointed time and place would have been difficult for him. I believe it had been getting increasingly difficult. And the day in question was the same day as the annual Blessing of the Animals at the Cathedral Church of Saint John the Divine, on

Amsterdam Avenue and 112th Street. Bowman was taking Snoot there, to be blessed.

Some misunderstanding occurred. Cathryn wanted to change the time of the rendezvous, I think, and telephoned to suggest it. She'd come a long distance, a Californian who rarely visited New York, and she was traveling with family. Bowman lived in New York, and had no children—surely it wasn't much to ask for him to emend a plan? Yet her proposal conflicted with Snoot's voyage to Harlem for the blessing. When Bowman presented this conflict, Cathryn, heartbreakingly for them both, teased him a little. His dog required blessing? So urgently he couldn't see her?

Cathryn, as one would expect, took Bowman's brilliant ironies, his tone of self-amused eccentricity and provocation, to mean he was capable of seeing himself in an absurd light. This was understandable—it was precisely what I'd done, falling in love with him long-distance, as I had. Yet there was nothing humorous about the blessing, from Bowman's side. California was a long way from New York, but for Bowman and Snoot, the ride to Harlem from the Lower East Side might have been equivalent.

Bowman, on the telephone, flipped his lid. Bowman blew his stack. It was a perfect misunderstanding, between two strangers who'd been jollied into conjunction by a go-between—me, that is. I doubt they ever did meet. Likely that day was the last time they spoke or e-mailed. But they both telephoned me, in a spirit of injury—Bowman enraged, as though his dog had again been attacked, kicked at on the street by an officious passerby, and Cathryn, on her side, utterly confused and appalled.

The slow degradation, and long shame, was mine. There came what we now call a tipping point—well, it was a tipping point for a lot of things—9/11. Bowman adopted the view that black helicopters had surveyed the scene minutes before the first airplane's impact. Disarranged by the fear that gripped us all during those Anthrax weeks that followed, but with fewer regular human contacts to provide solace, Bowman's self-skepticism betrayed him totally. On his favorite instrument, the telephone, he plagued a magazine editor with his paranoid theories concerning the attack. She was not only one of the last editors regularly commissioning pieces from him, one of the last bridges he'd failed to burn, she was one of my oldest friends. She complained to me, rightly—I'd put them together.

This, and other less flamboyant confusions, estranged us. I guess I couldn't take it, and I put Bowman on a kind of management course of contact and encouragement, as if Sarge had turned into a kind of methadone nurse. It wasn't necessary to exile him; he'd done it himself supremely well, as though systematically. By the time Bowman died our contacts were sporadic, our phone calls brief, and it had been years since he'd mailed me a charm. I'd quit having to defend him, or having to decide not to, to other writers, because other writers weren't raising his name to me. Either Bowman was reaching outside of his keep less frequently, or he wasn't dropping my name when he did. Likely some of both was the case. There wasn't anything Furry about this situation in the least.

## 14. Shit before Truck

There was a deeper trauma in David Bowman, something predating the Montauk Truck. The real shit on Bowman's shoes when he walked through the door of adult life was a thing barely revealed, a darkness in his childhood. This wasn't a story he retailed, a play he made for sympathy. When he told me the story, it wasn't really a story at all but a single image.

I'd been pressing him to explain how he could go so long without contact with his living mother. My mother had died when I was a teenager, and I'd have given my right arm for one conversation with her in adulthood. In another sense I also identified with Bowman—in the wake of my mother's death, in my high school years, I'd left my siblings and my father behind. After one year of college I'd run west, like the characters in *Let the Dog Drive*. For much of my twenties I'd barely seen my family, and rarely called my father. Only now I was back in touch, and glad to be, and I thought Bowman should consider the cost to his life, and perhaps to his art, of the wall he'd placed between himself and his personal past.

That day I'd pushed him just enough. He laid one single card on the table to justify his ban. I don't remember the words he used; I remember his body, and the pantomime he offered me as he described the scene, a kind of somatic reenactment. His father had beaten him while his mother stood by and watched and did nothing, but the unforgettable detail, the story Bowman wanted to show me with his body, was that his father had beaten him, not once, but in a sustained way, *across the hood of the family car*. I never asked for more.

This is probably the place to say even more clearly that I have no authority to speak of these matters. I'm neither a member of David's surviving extended family nor his biographer. My only claim is the memoirist's: these things happened to *me*, and I'm telling them to you as I recall them. I'll draw a curtain now on any further speculations (some may think I should have drawn a curtain sooner). The fact is, I had my own Bowman, and for most of a decade, since the brief flare of remembrances that accompanied the appearance of his obituary in the *New York Times*, I felt pretty certain I'd be alone with him for as long as I lived, and then he'd be gone. I never once expected that I'd try to give him to *you*.

## 15. The Big Bang

When the editor Judith Clain approached me—it was at another literary gala, one of those things I'm routinely invited to and David Bowman never was—and told me Little, Brown was to publish *Big Bang*, I couldn't have been more astonished if you'd hit me with, well, a truck. It was only then that understood not only that Bowman had finished his most improbable work, but that his talent wasn't my private possession, to be marveled at and pitied in my secret garden, but that it belonged, would now belong, to any reader who cared to pick it up. The kinky adoration he was able to lavish on the cultural materials he picked up and looked at in his books—the way he makes, for instance, Jackie Onassis into a very Furry character indeed, was never exclusively mine to know. Bowman is a language dervish—the pleasure in hearing him describe the adding machine, the source of William S. Burroughs's family fortune, as "the rosary of capitalism," belongs not to me but to literature.

*Big Bang* isn't a place to go for straight facts about the Kennedy assassination—as if there are "straight facts" about it!—nor is it a place to go for a philosophical fugue on the instability of conspiracy theories, in the manner of DeLillo's *Libra*. Indeed, though Bowman's book is full of facts, none of them are to be considered strictly reliable. When you learn, for instance, that Jimi Hendrix's "first electric guitar was a Supro Ozark. It was white plastic with a black headstock. The white was known in the music-store business as 'mother-of-toilet-seat finish,'" you will only have yourself or Google to trust, and who can trust Google? In this opus David Bowman has written a vast docu-fiction, one in which facts have been fused in the Ekco Hi-Speed Calrod Pressure Cooker of his imagination into something stranger and deeper—a psychic X-ray of the century previous to this one, an enlivening dream voyage into the mystery of the world that made ours and which still haunts it.

None of it is mine, really, to defend or explain. I'm just Bowman's reader now, like you. It only happened that I had a front-row seat to a show I never believed could open, and now has opened.

What belongs to me are the tapes.

# Snowden in the Labyrinth
Review of *Permanent Record* by Edward
Snowden (Metropolitan Books, 2019)

## 1. A Moment of Vision

In Robert Sheckley's 1978 short story "Is *That* What People Do?" a man named Eddie Quintero buys himself a pair of binoculars from an army and navy surplus outlet, "because with them he hoped to see some things that he otherwise would never see. Specifically, he hoped to see girls undressing at the Chauvin Arms across the street from his furnished room"—but he was also "looking for that moment of vision, of total attention." Since this is a science fiction story, Quintero accidentally ends up with a pair marked "Experimental. Not to be removed from the Testing Room."

The binoculars turn out to have a spectacular capacity not only for seeing through walls, but also for diminishing the distance between Quintero and those he would spy on. When he peers through the experimental device *just so*—an effort of contorting his body into increasingly bizarre positions—Quintero is suddenly granted visions of other human beings, behind closed doors, doing "what people do." Which turns out to be, well, weird shit. The least disturbing of what Quintero surveils is what's now called cosplay; the most extreme consists of giddy ritual murder, and of the deliberate calling-forth of a satanic, sexually violent "smoke demon." On the last page, Sheckley's parable attains an existential-ist clarity: the binoculars grant a vision of a shabby, middle-aged man in a barely furnished room, standing on his head, with a pair of binoculars awkwardly wedged against his face. Quintero recognizes himself:

> He realized that he was only another performer in human-ity's great circus, and he had just done one of his acts, just like the others. But who was watching? Who was the real observer?
>
> He turned the binoculars around and looked through the object-lenses. He saw a pair of eyes, and he thought they were his own—until one of them slowly winked at him.

Edward Snowden, late in the pages in his memoir, *Permanent Record*, describes his sensation at being personally introduced to XKEYSCORE, the NSA's ultimate tool of intimate, individual electronic surveillance. Among the NSA's technological tools (some of which Snowden aided in perfecting), XKEYSCORE was, according to Snowden, "the most invasive . . . if only because [the NSA agents are] closest to the user—that is, the closest to the per-son being surveilled." For nearly three hundred pages, the memoir has built to this scene, foreshadowed in the preface, in which the whistleblower-in-the-making sees behind the curtain:

> I sat at a terminal from which I had practically unlimited access to the communications of nearly every man, woman,

and child on earth who'd ever dialed a phone or touched a computer. Among those people were about 320 million of my fellow American citizens, who in the regular conduct of their everyday lives were being surveilled in gross contravention of not just the Constitution of the United States, but the basic values of any free society.

The steady approach to Snowden's come-to-Jesus encounter with XKEYSCORE is as meticulous as the incremental unveiling of the terror of Cthulhu in an H.P. Lovecraft tale. Snowden himself alludes to this parallel:

> It was, simply put, the closest thing to science fiction I've ever seen in science fact: an interface that allows you to type in pretty much anyone's address, telephone number, or IP address, and then basically go through the recent history of their online activity. In some cases you could even play back recordings of their online sessions, so that the screen you'd be looking at was their screen, whatever was on their desktop.

And: "It was like watching an autocomplete, as letters and words flashed across the screen . . . but the intelligence behind that typing wasn't artificial but human: this was a humancomplete." And:

> One thing you come to understand very quickly while using XKEYSCORE is that nearly anyone in the world who's

online has at least two things in common: they have all watched porn at one time or another, and they all store photos and videos of their family. This was true for virtually everyone of every gender, ethnicity, race, and age—from the meanest terrorist to the nicest senior citizen.

The *humancomplete* that chills Snowden's blood is "this one child in particular, a little boy in Indonesia. Technically, I shouldn't have been interested in this little boy, but I was, because my employers were interested in his father" (who was, according to Snowden, "just a regular academic who'd been caught up in a surveillance dragnet"):

He was sitting in front of his computer, as I was sitting in front of mine. Except that in his lap he had a toddler, a boy in his diaper.

The father was trying to read something, but the kid kept shifting around, smacking the keys and giggling. The computer's internal mic picked up his giggling and there I was, listening to it on my headphones. The father held the boy tighter, and the boy straightened up, and, with his dark crescent eyes, looked directly into the computer's camera—I couldn't escape the feeling that he was looking directly at me. Suddenly I realized that I'd been holding my breath.

*Permanent Record* is an attempt to reverse the binoculars and offer a self-portrait of the man—whistleblower? leaker? dissident?

spy?—who walks the earth, these days in Moscow, under the name Edward Snowden.

Snowden might seem forever defined by a single act—his decision to leak highly classified information copied from the NSA—and a single moment in time. Having gazed through the windows of the panopticon, he experienced that rarity, a moment of vision: *the world must be told these things I know*. Against absurd odds, he delivered his knowledge to us. Now, he proposes to explain to you, by first explaining to himself, how he became (both how he was formed and why he chose to become) the person playing this watershed walk-on part on the recent historical stage.

If the reader gauges this prospect with resistance (Didn't I see a fine documentary on this subject, several years back? Didn't I read somewhere that Snowden's a nonentity?), it is mirrored in Snowden's own doubts:

> The fact is, no one with a biography like mine ever comes comfortably to autobiography. It's hard to have spent so much of my life trying to avoid identification, only to turn around completely and share "personal disclosures" in a book. The Intelligence Community tries to inculcate in its workers a baseline anonymity, a sort of blank-page personality upon which to inscribe secrecy and the art of imposture.

Snowden goes further in describing the conundrum he faces, comparing the process of self-erosion typical in his chosen field of spycraft to the task of data encryption he was hired to do: "As in any process of encryption, the original material—your core identity—still exists, but only in a locked and scrambled form."

Do we need a memoir by a person who proposes that "the more you know about others, the less you know about yourself?" Perhaps, if we grant that Snowden's difficulty may not be the exclusive province of spies, but rather embodies a characteristic fissure in contemporary selfhood.

## 2. Free Country

Snowden's book is straightforward, admirably so. He has taken the risk of assuming that his reader is interested not only in his "moment of vision" and the brazen act that earned his fame and notoriety, but also in the formation of his personality, and the slow growth of his understanding of technology, espionage, surveillance, and human rights. Despite his gifts at computer programming, he has no interest in persuading you that he's unusual; quite the opposite. A clean-cut, apolitical child of a military family, his father a Coast Guard officer, his mother a federal employee—his parents divorced in 2001—Snowden is a gentle and conforming type, and he's consistently amazed that more people don't feel as he does about the intelligence community's crimes. He walks us through his self-indoctrination in that community, his fascinatingly bland career in and around the CIA and NSA, his strangely easy location of a loyal life partner (he and his wife, Lindsay, met—you guessed it—online), and the steady growth of his disappointment with the ethical compasses of those around and above him, including President Obama.

His memoir is also a before-and-after account of 9/11. Here again, his book succeeds in the act of earnest witnessing. His vantage is remarkable: the sixteen-year-old computing prodigy had taken a job, assisting in a private Web design company run out of a private house that happens to be situated within the boundary of the NSA's home military base:

> It's nearly inconceivable now, but at the time Fort Meade was almost entirely accessible to anyone. It wasn't all bollards and barricades and checkpoints trapped in barbed wire. It could just drive onto the army base housing the world's most secretive intelligence agency in my '92 Civic, windows down, radio up, without having to stop at a gate and show ID. . . . It seemed like every other weekend or so a quarter of my Japanese class would congregate in Mae's little house behind NSA headquarters to watch anime and create comics. That's just the way it was, in those bygone days when "It's a free country, isn't it?" was a phrase you heard in every schoolyard and sitcom.

Cut to:

> Pandemonium, chaos: our most ancient forms of terror. . . . For as long as I live, I'll remember retracing my way up Canine Road—the road past the NSA's headquarters—after the Pentagon was attacked. Madness poured out of the agency's black glass towers, a tide of yelling, ringing cell

phones, and cars revving up in the parking lots and fighting their way onto the streets. At the moment of the worst terrorist attack in American history, the staff of the NSA—the major signals agency of the American IC—was abandoning its work by the thousands, and I was swept up in the flood.

After the September 11 attacks, Snowden—"obediently following along in, in what today I recall as one totalizing moment"—was set on his patriotic course: enlistment in the Army (followed, after an injury, by a neutral form of discharge known as "administrative separation"), then the search for high-level government clearance, in order to offer his computing skills in the intelligence community marketplace. The CIA and NSA usually hire people with talents like Snowden's as federally cleared private contractors, rather than directly conscripting them to one of the agencies. Snowden walks us through this baroque arrangement, which arises primarily as a budgeting workaround; implicit is a defense against any dismissals of his role on the grounds that he was "merely a contractor."

If you choose to believe this memoir—I do—then that same unironic patriotic nerve drove each subsequent phase of Snowden's disillusioning, and what followed: the iconoclastic deed that propelled him to fame. The flavor of Snowden's account is *nerd ingenuous*. He strings together remarks that can seem awfully obvious, but that gain in cumulative effect:

> To hack a system requires getting to know its rules better than the people who created it or are running it.

The computer guy knows everything, or rather can know everything.

> I occupied one of the most unexpectedly omniscient positions in the Intelligence Community—toward the bottom rung of the managerial ladder, but high atop heaven in terms of access.
>
> At the time I didn't realize that engineering a system that would keep a permanent record of everyone's life was a tragic mistake.

Sometimes he generates an eerie koan:

> Deletion has never existed.

Speaking of the commonalities between the Intelligence Community and the tech industry:

> Both are entrenched and unelected powers that pride themselves on maintaining absolute secrecy about their developments. Both believe they have the solutions for everything, which they never hesitate to unilaterally impose. Above all, they both believe that these solutions are inherently apolitical, because they're based on data.

And, after a long contemplation of the painful losses of US lives on 9/11, this bare remark: "Over one million people have been killed in the course of American's response."

How does one decide to become the dissident, the scapegoat, the whistleblower? Snowden seems as mystified as we are. It is as if one day the question simply appears, fully formed: Why am *I* the one who cares? Why am I haunted by the eyes of the boy in his father's lap while other operatives with access to XKEYSCORE are busy collecting nudes and stalking ex-girlfriends? (Alas, yes. They even have a nickname for it: LOVEINT, a satirical variation on HUMINT and SIGINT—human and signals intelligence.) "To whom could I turn?" he writes. "Who could I talk to? Even to whisper the truth, even to a lawyer or judge or to Congress, had been made so severe a felony that just a basic outlining of the broadest facts would invite a lifetime sentence in a federal cell."

Snowden suffers as he privately traces the extent of the crimes and realizes the deceptions required to carry them out. He twists through feelings of shame at his complicity; astonishment at the indifference around him; fear at the onset of loneliness, a loneliness he knows is only a sneak preview of the isolations awaiting him if he acts. There's also a sort of bargaining and denial phase, as he assesses whether he's too lowly to play the part in which he's cast himself: "Who'd elected me the president of secrets?"

Yet the answer is as plain as the publication date of his book: September 17, Constitution Day. (Disclosure: I'd never heard of it.) Snowden's a Constitution dork. He's the one guy in the office who actually takes a copy of the document off the "free table"; he's the one guy who actually reads it. He *likes* reading it, "partially because its ideas are great, partially because its prose is good, but really because it freaked out my coworkers."

My theory is that with that last line Snowden is trying to laugh away the pain. I believe the Constitution—particularly the Bill of Rights— became, for Snowden, a kind of lonely companion, or perhaps something like a rescue animal that only he cares for sufficiently. In the period in which he's struggling to understand whether it is incumbent on him to destroy his life to protect the Constitution, Snowden is diagnosed with epilepsy. Though he himself never quite goes there, it's hard not to interpret these chapters allegorically: cognitive dissonance as a slow-motion brain seizure. Secrecy as disease.

### 3. Chain of Command

In his *New Yorker* essay "The Outside Man," Malcolm Gladwell made a disappointed comparison between Daniel Ellsberg—the eloquent, Vietnam War–era leaker of the Pentagon Papers—and Edward Snowden:

> Ellsberg was handsome and charismatic. . . . He did his undergraduate and graduate studies at Harvard, where he wrote a Ph.D. dissertation on game theory and collaborated with Thomas Schelling, who went on to win a Nobel Prize. He took a senior post in McNamara's Defense Department, represented the State Department in Vietnam, and had two stints as a senior intelligence analyst at the RAND Corporation.

When he encountered evidence of the Johnson administration's deceptions about the Vietnam War, Ellsberg first "went to the Senate, where he tried to get someone to release the documents formally and hold public hearings," and even tried to interest his friend and mentee Henry Kissinger. Having become disillusioned with his options within the halls of government, Ellsberg leaks, but only within what Gladwell dubs, in a pregnant phrase, "the norms of insider disclosure":

> And whom does [Ellsberg] entrust with those forty-three volumes? The *Times*, which rents a suite at the Hilton, posts security guards outside, and assigns a team to spend the next three months reading through the collected documents. . . . Would the *Times* have won a Pulitzer for publishing the Pentagon Papers if the study had been unclassified? Not a chance.

Harvard, Nobel, RAND, Pulitzer, the *Times*, *and* the Hilton—oh my! Gladwell's nostalgia for the Cold War–era social order squats over this account, as candid as it is unexamined. By this standard, Ellsberg's successor isn't up to snuff:

> Snowden did not study under a Nobel Prize winner, or give career advice to the likes of Henry Kissinger. He was a community-college dropout, a member of the murky hacking counterculture. . . . The élites, Snowden once said, "know everything about us and we know nothing about them— because they are secret, they are privileged, and they are a separate class.

Gladwell quotes this without the slightest concern for self-incrimination. He goes on:

> Information—particularly sensitive information—has a pedigree. . . . The relationship between the government and the press—between the source of leaks and the beneficiary of leaks—is symbiotic . . . When I worked on the science desk at the *Washington Post*, my colleagues and I would read a front-page story by our counterparts at the *Times* and invariably know where the leak on which the story was based came from. The first order of business was to call the leaker and complain that he or she was playing favorites.

Symbiotic—that's one word for it. Cozy, elite, secret—others. Gladwell ends by chiding Snowden for not having seen Kubrick's *Dr. Strangelove*; along with everything else, measured against worldly Ellsberg, Snowden's just no fun.

In *Permanent Record*, Edward Snowden doesn't say whether he cares what the *New Yorker*'s readers think of his knowledge of 1960s cinema, but he explains why he didn't turn to the *New York Times*. It's not a social matter:

> Whenever I thought about contacting the *Times*, I found myself hesitating. While the paper had shown some willingness to displease the US government with its WikiLeaks reporting, I couldn't stop reminding myself of its earlier conduct involving an important article on the government's

warrantless wiretapping program by Eric Lichtblau and James Risen. These two journalists . . . had managed to uncover one aspect of STELLARWIND—the NSA's original-recipe post 9/11 surveillance initiative—and had produced a fully written, edited, and fact-checked article about it, ready to go to press by mid-2004. It was at this point that the paper's editor in chief, Bill Keller, ran the article past the government, as part of a courtesy process. . . . If the *Times*, or any paper, did something similar to me . . . it would be tantamount to turning me in before any revelations were brought before the public.

Interestingly, Snowden declines to make direct comparison between his assessment of the Fourth Estate and another concern in his book: the military's imperative to stay within "the chain of command." What if the whistleblower wishes to expose the person directly above them? What if it is *precisely* your immediate superior who is unreliable, corrupt? Is the chain of command corrupt as well? Essentially, the problem Snowden faced with his direct military superiors was the same he faced in considering mainstream journalism: the chain of command might function as a trap for heretics.

Meanwhile, Ellsberg—who, when I used to meet him at the counter of used bookstores where I worked in Berkeley in the 1980s, seemed very much the canny old hippie—has, since his ejection from the corridors of power, dedicated his life to activism against US military interventions; been arrested in multiple nonviolent protests; spoken in support of Julian Assange, Chelsea Manning, and Snowden; and camped on Sproul Plaza during the Occupy movement. That's the same Sproul Plaza, of course, that gave a stage to Free Speech Movement activist Mario Savio in 1964: "There is a time when the operation of the machine becomes so odious, makes you so sick at heart, that you can't take part."

## 4. Something with Eyes

In her remarkable new collection *Trick Mirror*, Jia Tolentino meditates on the internet's potential for the destruction of our sense of scale:

> Like many of us, I have become acutely conscious of the way my brain degrades when I strap it in to receive the full barrage of the internet—those unlimited channels, all constantly reloading with new information: births, deaths, boasts, bombings, jokes, job announcements, ads, warnings, complaints, confessions, and political disasters blitzing our frayed neurons in huge waves of information that pummel us and then are instantly replaced.

As Tolentino paints it, this is an experience defined by its paralyzing incoherence. If the "feed" presents as an ocean of injustices, of rival neglected crises, it is also one salted through with rival dismissive claims, and with shaming scorn, and outright lies. All this, plus clickable icons relentlessly shaped to trigger irruptions from one's lizard appetites for orgasm, revenge, and gossip.

As for the constants of surveillance and self-surveillance, these end in stalemate. Or perhaps it is a form of Stockholm Syndrome, of learned helplessness. In my own half-assed survey, nearly anyone, reminded of the facts of either corporate or NSA command of their data and metadata, tends to exhibit a throb of outrage, swiftly followed by a shrug of resigned, ironized acceptance: *Sure, that happened, but me, I've got nothing to hide.* Or: *I was on their watch-list anyway.* Or: *It often recommends bands I wouldn't have known about!* Snowden's implicit question, throughout his book, is: Why can't I make people care?

I was born in 1964. Some of my favorite books attempt an accounting of what life was like before, during, and after some large rupture in the collective human prospect, or the advent of a reality-reshaping paradigm, ideology, or technology. Transformations still in living memory, but receding fast: Anthony Powell's *A Dance to the Music of Time,* Robert Musil's *The Man Without Qualities,* Doris Lessing's *The Children of Violence,* Ford Madox Ford's *Parade's End*—each of which try to encompass the atmospheric changes between and around convulsive European wars, as does Paul Fussell's tremendous study, *The Great War and Modern Memory.* Booth Tarkington's *The Magnificent Ambersons* partly concerns itself with the effect of coming of the automobile on small-town midwestern life. George W.S. Trow's glinting essay "Within the Context of No Context" captures television's insidious displacement of older social orders.

Earlier, I had gobbled up postwar US science fiction, making it a permanent lens for my own fumbling understanding of the world (as I've made obvious in this essay). Much of that writing, especially the 1950s writers clustered around *Galaxy* magazine, Sheckley among them, now looks to me like thought experiments for a society overwhelmed—intoxicated and traumatized, both—by the advent of radio, television, rocketry, Madison Avenue, and nuclear war. Overwhelmed, too, by the vertiginous growth of a thing that had not yet gained the name "globalized corporate capitalism." It strikes me now that the intricate ruminations of those long historical fictions, and the short sharp shocks of science fiction—the literature of "cognitive estrangement"—are both making the same implicit claim: that after the accelerating transformations of the nineteenth and twentieth centuries, you can't really ponder being alive in the twenty-first merely by describing the present. That's because the present doesn't exist.

I now teach writing to people much younger than myself—to the children of the internet and the post-9/11 security state and triumphalist global corporatism and climate doom. It's a truism already to say they read (and watch, and write) dystopian stories because they're living in one. No surprise, they've got little time for Lessing or Ford; those transitions are too deep in the rear-view mirror. The majority of my students find little nourishment in the placid assumptions underlying contemporary realism. They crave acknowledgement, not that the world has changed, or is changing, but that the world *is* change.

I think direct testimony also plays well these days, for my young students, for a lot of us. Self-scrupulousness in prose, when it is as exacting as Tolentino's, both excites and calms because it places a pin the one thing we can safely say about the "now": that each of us is working hard to handle it. Snowden, for his part, offers a meticulous and expressive description of the advent, in his young life, of computing, and the seductions of the virtual:

> This Compac [computer] became my constant companion—my second sibling, and first love. It came into my life just at the age when I was first discovering an independent self and the multiple worlds that can simultaneously exist within this world. . . . This was a technologized puberty, and the tremendous changes it wrought in me were, in a way, being wrought everywhere, in everyone. . . . With just this cord, the Compac's expansion card and modem, and a working phone, I could dial up and connect to something new called the Internet. . . . Readers who were born postmillennium might not understand the fuss, but trust me, this was a goddamned miracle. . . . You could pick up any other phone in the house on an extension line and actually *hear the computers talking*. . . . Internet access, and the emergence of the Web, was my generation's big bang or Precambrian explosion. . . . I sometimes had the feeling that I had to know everything and wasn't going to sign off until I did. It was like I was in a race with the technology.

And:

> How can I explain it, to someone who wasn't there? My younger readers, with their younger standards, might think of the nascent Internet as way too slow, the nascent Web as too ugly and un-entertaining. But that would be wrong. Back then, being online was another life, considered by most to be separate and distinct from Real Life. The virtual and the actual had not yet merged. And it was up to each individual user to determine for themselves where one ended and the other began.

While both Tolentino and Snowden wax nostalgic for an earlier version of the internet, it's hardly clear they're talking about exactly the same thing. Snowden (born 1983) specifically credits anonymity with the liberatory power of the early Web:

> One of the greatest joys of these platforms was that on them I didn't have to be who I was. I could be anybody. The anonymizing or pseudonymizing features brought equilibrium to all relationships, correcting their imbalances. . . . I could even be multiple selves. . . . In the 1990s, the Internet had yet to fall victim to the greatest iniquity in digital history: the move by government and businesses to link, as intimately as possible, users' online personas to their offline legal identity . . . enforcing fidelity to memory, identarian consistency, and so ideological conformity.

Though Snowden isn't prone to philosophical citation, his sentiment here is Nietzschean: "Rather than making oneself uniform," Nietzsche wrote in *Human, All Too Human*, "we may find greater value for the enrichment of knowledge by listening to the soft voice of different life situations; each brings its own views with it. Thus we acknowledge and share the life and nature of many by not treating ourselves like rigid, invariable, single individuals."

Tolentino (born 1988) associates anonymity with nihilism and bullying. Her perspective is more inflected than Snowden's; ambivalent about the inflation of the value of a stabilized "real" identity online, she's marvelously even-tempered about online trolls:

> The rise of trolling, and its ethos of disrespect and anonymity, has been so forceful in part because of the internet's insistence on consistent, approval-worthy identity is so strong. . . . My only experience of the world has been one in which personal appeal is paramount and self-exposure is encouraged; this legitimately unfortunate paradigm, inhabited first by women and now generalized to the entire internet, is what trolls loathe and actively repudiate. They destabilize an internet built on transparency and likeability.

Part of this difference is gendered: Snowden, as a man, can afford a certain obliviousness to all the stalking and doxxing, since most of it is aimed at women. Anyway, by the time of the "curdling of the social internet" (Tolentino's words; she dates it to

2012), Snowden had long since vanished into his own spook's labyrinth of alterna-nets and crypto-webs. By his testimony, the CIA even maintains a completely separate version of Facebook for the socializing of agents. Snowden's bitterness at the loss of his childhood playground is also his warning to us: the famous *New Yorker* cartoon—"On the internet, nobody knows you're a dog"—has been exposed as naïve. Snowden wants us to understand that, unless you employ three-layer encryption, they even know your breed.

His descriptions are in no way redundant to Tolentino's, even if they're rather specialized. We'll need more of these; out of an accumulation of intimate accounts, a picture of this age will emerge. If one is possible. The internet, like climate change, exemplifies what Timothy Morton has dubbed "a hyperobject": a thing impossible to hold in mind because of its context-smashing extensivity in time and space (or 'space'). In *Lurking: How a Person Became a User*, Joanne McNeil (born 1980) writes from the point of view of an internet "supertaster," a veteran of more platforms and forums and flame wars and start-ups than I—or, possibly, even Tolentino—could ever wish to endure. She immerses herself in the paradoxes of an experience that relentlessly exfoliates metaphor: "People used to talk about the internet as a place. The information superhighway. A frontier. The internet was something to get on. . . . Now people talk about the internet as something to talk to; it is a someone. Even casually, people discuss the internet—insentient, dumb—as living, real. A friend or foe. Something with eyes."

## 5. Giving Up the Gun

McNeil, talking of what she calls "the deliquescence of the early internet," explains its upside:

> Truly rotten racist trolls online were free to ruin communities. . . . However, the scope of their abuse was curtailed by the limits of the services and data available: communicating username to username, your real life remained private—a troll couldn't send nasty emails to your boss or threaten your parents, let alone have a SWAT team dispatched to your front door. . . . A user could wake up one morning, delete a newsgroup subscription from their Usenet client, and go about the rest of their life never talking to that community again. You couldn't look up old ghosts on Instagram or find them through search engines. These anonymous users walked back into the ether where they came from.

At the other end of this story, Snowden and Lindsay are shopping for kitchenware, when he spots a refrigerator:

> It was a "Smart-fridge," which was being advertised as "Internet-equipped." . . . You could check your email, or check your calendar. You could watch YouTube clips, or listen to MP3s. You could even make phone calls. I had to restrain myself from keying in Lindsay's number and saying, from across the floor, "I'm calling from a fridge." . . . The fridge's computer kept track of internet temperature, and,

through scanning barcodes, the freshness of your food. It also provided nutritional information. . . . I remember driving home in confused silence. . . . The only reason the thing was Internet-equipped was so that it could report back to its manufacturer about its owner's usage and about any other household data that was obtainable. The manufacturer, in turn, would monetize that data by selling it. And we were supposed to pay for the privilege.

I wondered what the point was of my getting so worked up over government surveillance if my friends, neighbors, and fellow citizens were more than happy to invite corporate surveillance into their homes. . . . I imagined the future SmartFridge stationed in my kitchen, monitoring my conduct and habits, and using my tendency to drink straight from the carton or not wash my hands to evaluate the probability of my being a felon.<sup>*</sup>

Or, in another of Snowden's koans, "Your possessions would possess you." It's not only that the "user"—the human, that is—can no longer shut the lid of the networked computer, in favor of a return to "the real world." Now, the user invites the computer, with its power to surveil and enthrall, to invest in every possible form of tool or furnishing, the simple and unsimple: socks, books,

---

\*    In the game of "Which Philip K. Dick Story Are We in Today?" (https://fraser.typepad.com/frolix_8/2015/06/which-pkd-story-are-we-in-today.html), Snowden's fridge fantasy is "Minority Report."

houses, watches, medical and fitness devices, and, of course, telephones. This trajectory is seen as irreversible. Here's Tolentino:

> I'll admit that I'm not sure that this inquiry is even productive. The internet reminds us on a daily basis that it is not at all rewarding to become aware of problems that you have no reasonable hope of solving. And, more important, the internet already is what it is. It has already become the central organ of contemporary life.

And back to Snowden:

> Technology doesn't have a Hippocratic oath . . . the intention driving a technology's invention rarely, if ever, limits its application and use. . . . I do not mean, of course, to compare nuclear weapons with cybersurveillance in terms of human cost. But there is a commonality when it comes to the concepts of proliferation and disarmament.

In his 1979 book *Giving Up the Gun: Japan's Reversion to the Sword, 1543–1879*, Noel Perrin describes an epoch in which a technologically sophisticated Japanese culture at least temporarily suppressed the flintlock rifle, preferring to revert to what they viewed as a more honorable, less inhuman manner of conducting war. Perrin's book doubles as a wishful allegory of the dream of nuclear disarmament. Perhaps it is time to update Fredric Jameson's famous quip, "It is easier to imagine the end of the world than to imagine the end of capitalism": Do we even have the power to dream of some kind of limitation to the colonization of our hours and days, our subjective and intersubjective spaces, by Snowden's fridge? The other day I heard a conversation on NPR about what gender we ought to use in addressing household robots, like Amazon's Alexa. That we'd *need* to address—her? him? them?— was the conversation's unstated assumption.

Fantasizing about disconnection is a privilege. That's already proven by the existence of off-the-grid luxury resorts, on remote islands in the Caribbean and Seychelles Islands, or tucked away in continental North America under names like Amangira and Amuleto. There'll be more like this, I wager. Short of such indulgence, many depend on connection for their livelihoods, or for their only affordable access to reading or research, as well as for a realm of social and cultural practice in a nation with a depraved indifference to the value of a "public commons." Many thousands, if not millions, of marginalized, isolated people may owe their very lives to social media; certainly we all owe it much of the present visibility and solidarity of the LGBTQ movement, and others. The history of social media is the story of the Arab Spring, of Occupy, of Barack Obama's election. I suppose it is also the story of some other things, too.

## 6. Citizenfour

*Permanent Record* peaks a bit earlier than Snowden thinks, and than the reader might expect. The intimate drama of his discoveries and self-discoveries, of the inception of his appetite for virtuality and for systems, of the rise of his patriotism in both its early-naïve and late-embittered phases, of his minor adventures as an ordinary operative with an extraordinary mind, and, above all, the helpless formation of his ethical crisis—these make terrific reading. What a strangely ordinary man: Snowden's either the least enigmatic cipher or the most gnomic nonentity ever to live. You could watch him study himself forever.

Yet from the moment Snowden hits the public sphere, the book wilts. The last few chapters are a blur of lawyers and airports, until in desperation the fugitive hands the book off to the reactions of his dismayed girlfriend, Lindsay. One feels that from the instant Snowden opens the door to the Hong Kong hotel and decants himself to Glenn Greenwald and Laura Poitras—whose documentary, *Citizenfour*, enshrines that very moment in real time—he's a ghost in his own tale. From that point, Greenwald's narrative—decisions about disclosures, partnerships with other journalistic institutions, and so forth—would be far more interesting.

The only remaining drama is that of the body's survival, and its loneliness. The last sequence of Poitras's movie is heartbreaking. Already, in the film, he's been reduced to the status of listener, as others describe to him the cascading consequences of his act, the grim machinations he's both revealed and triggered. He was a man who had just one thing to tell us, really. He did tell it, and some listened, and some believed, and others didn't. The fever is now broken.

The book takes beyond this point, to his landing in Moscow. There's no next move except to hunker down and hope for a reunion with Lindsay. Mercifully, she shows up. They visit an art museum. One feels, sadly, that if only he could be not only forgiven, but rehired by the NSA, he'd be just the guy to repair the technical mess the other, earlier guy named Edward Snowden left behind. He'd do a good job. He's the computer guy.

# The Collapsing Frontier

**Wide Load / "Mr. Blue Sky"**

The characters ride into the story aboard a 1984 Winnebago Minnie Winnie, one driven breakneck across broiling asphalt, overspilling its lane on both sides. Though the story's characters are themselves oblivious, the story acknowledges that it is being written on stolen Tongva land—indeed, the same Tongva land toward which the recreational vehicle now barrels. The story gives respect and reverence to those who came before it, which ought to be absolutely everyone, even you, reader, since the story does not yet and may never exist. Yet here it seems to come—the story, and the recreational vehicle—the Winnebago like a breadbox rumbling westward on fat half-melted tires, a monster's breadbox with its bragging orange stripe, side-view mirrors flying-buttressed a full foot from its cab to make it minimally navigable. The story already occupies too much space, demands too much attention. What the fuck, watch where you're going! Who's driving that thing? A dad in mirrored aviator shades? Why, of course. He's Robert Crumb's Whiteman, he's Albert Brooks in *Lost in America*, he's the Exhausted Normative Protagonist—our movie's leading man, there's no way to avoid him. Or maybe there is. Maybe one of his kids or his long-suffering wife can provide us with a marginally improved point of view, a parallax position from which to operate. Some fucking oxygen here, though it may be that all the oxygen is recirculated within the tightly sealed Winnebago. They all breathe the same air, surely. At least we can't hear the music inside: Electric Light Orchestra's *Greatest Hits*, on 8-track tape.

## The Story's Writer / "Turn to Stone"

The alternative is equally unpromising: that we raise up a literary selfie stick and catch a glimpse of the story's writer. We might choose to cast him as the protagonist in a drama of the story's becoming (or, more likely, of the story's failure to launch, burdened as it is with debts and doubts, with qualms and queasy self-loathing). Of course, and it goes without saying, the story's writer is also male and white—another exemplar of the Exhausted Normative. And the project of literary self-consciousness is hardly novel (a pun, there), since it has been indulged by so many of the writer's immediate and distant influences, from Kurt Vonnegut and Philip K. Dick to Jorge Luis Borges and Laurence Sterne. This model of self-consciousness has lately been renovated, refurbished, under the name "autofiction," yet even so it may be once again an expiring mode. Sure, it offers itself as an exit from the interstate freeway of narrative—the kind of storytelling that doesn't trouble over the existence of the author, just barrels ever forward, claiming the turf of your attention. But perhaps it has proved to be an exit that is closed for repairs or has simply shut down because no one wishes to go there anymore.

Among those who may wish to avoid self-consciousness: the writer of this story. The writer wants to fight to stay on the interstate freeway of storytelling! He wants to get somewhere! He wants to be aboard the Winnebago!

If so, this is no way to go about it.

## Yet Further Disclaimers / "Can't Get It Out of My Head"

The story acknowledges borrowing the language of its acknowledgement of its occupation of stolen Tongva land from the website of a collective of spirit healers, who will go unnamed in this acknowledgement, for they may not wish to be associated. The story admits it also depends for its existence on an occupation of the text of R.A. Lafferty's "Narrow Valley," a text the story's author first encountered in the anthology *Other Dimensions*, edited by Robert Silverberg in 1973. The story takes place six years later, in 1979, the year of Three Mile Island, of the Iranian Hostage Crisis, of the imminence of the Reagan era. The feeling that the Reagan Era was coming is a migraine prodrome, a hangover suffered before a decades-long binge on Militarism, Bogus Optimism, and Imperial Fantasy that still hasn't abated. Since, really, what is the twenty-first century except the endless unspooling of the implications of the Reagan Era? But the writer digresses. The clown Emmett Kelly died in 1979, as did John Wayne and Jack Soo and Sid Vicious. Natasha Lyonne and Ben Lerner and Pink were born in 1979. The story now acknowledges consulting Wikipedia's "1979 in the United States" pages. But who is R.A. Lafferty? A writer of science fiction and westerns, Lafferty lived most of his life in Tulsa, Oklahoma. He died at eighty-seven in 2002. He was a Catholic. What's "Narrow Valley"? A short story that is both a science fiction story and a western story, as well as a kind of tall tale or parable, typical of Lafferty's eccentric style. In it a white family attempts to purchase—for back taxes—acreage originally given by the US government in a land allotment to a Pawnee Indian named Clarence Big-Saddle, and handed down to his son, Clarence Little-Saddle.

The land appears, from a distance, to be a broad and fertile valley, with an alluring topography. However, when the white family attempts to enter the valley, it reveals itself as a spatial anomaly—a strip of space between two fences which is too small to enter. Or, when a person such as the white family insists upon entering it, it shrinks and flattens them to fit. The story, published in 1966, still has much to recommend it: a delightful insouciance; admirable ethics (even if expressed in twentieth-century terms); surrealist humor; a winking self-awareness that affiliates it with more labored forms of literary metafiction yet lacking in the overt self-consciousness with which the present story is hobbled. The story now acknowledges that by basing itself on a specific earlier short science fiction story it is also indebted, paradoxically, to another: "The Nine Billion Names of God," by Carter Scholz, which bases itself on "The Nine Billion Names of God" by Arthur C. Clarke, and which has amused and obsessed the writer of the present story for decades. Carter Scholz is a friend of the writer of the story; the present story waves to Carter from the window of a passing Winnebago, as it hurtles in the direction of Lafferty's impossible valley. The story now acknowledges its utter colonization by its own procedure of confession of sources. The story, which initially believed itself to be operating on a blank page, moving into a horizon of possibility, is dismayed by the possibility that it has wandered instead into a sucking undertow of bungled authorial good intentions, the pathetic desire to write a story that will acknowledge its colonial crimes and historical debts. The Winnebago, moving with such innocent optimism across deserted western spaces, may be blundering into a valley of palimpsest. The story is belated.

## Collapsing Frontier / "Strange Magic"

The man and wife and kids in the Winnebago are moving west. The story moves west with them. All stories around here move west. An exhausting procedure, but necessary. Frederick Jackson Turner made this inevitable with his "frontier thesis." Turner's thesis declares that white people placed their boot prints on the American continent in the name of a national idea. The thesis rationalized their push west as a noble effort to occupy land that was as good as waiting for them, like a medium waiting for the artistry of their realization. It claimed that the land lay waiting, as ready as a blank page, one on which new meaning could be sprinkled as easily as tapping at alphabetic keys, as the writer finds himself doing right now. This story has attempted to launch itself on a presumption of innocence: it shouldn't need to push another story off the page in order to be written, should it? It's not required that the story murder another story! Intertextuality isn't colonization!

Reference isn't smallpox! The Winnebago rumbles through open space, not an obstacle in sight. The man has purchased some desert land, sight unseen—acreage described to him by the realtor as "virgin." He and his family are driving there to claim it. We have to pretend this might work out for him and his family, even though we know it doesn't, whether we have read Lafferty's version or not. There are two names for this operation: Suspension of Disbelief and Bad Faith.

## An Indian / "Showdown"

The story is headed into crisis because the white family must—as in Lafferty's original—meet an Indian. A Native American. An Indigenous North American person. The difficulty in even producing even a stable term ("These terms have come in and out of favor over the years, and different tribes, not to mention different people, have different preferences. . . . A good rule of thumb for outsiders: Ask the Native people you're talking to what they prefer," David Treuer wrote, in *The Heartbeat of Wounded Knee*) shows how unlikely it is that the story's writer will be capable of manifesting such a character, or such a scene, on the page. Should we presume it was simpler for Lafferty? He would at least not have hesitated at calling the character an Indian. As a securely twentieth-century-situated human, one who lived almost his whole life in Tulsa, Lafferty imparted to characters such as Clarence Little-Saddle an air of fond and easeful familiarity. He employed Clarence Little-Saddle in the cause of punching up at the presumptions of the white characters, their avarice and delusions, as well as the garbled scientific pontification of the characters who were called in as experts to examine the paradox of the mysteriously narrow valley.

It will not be so simple for this story's writer. In his dismay he recalls some astounding advice—a "craft tip"—he absorbed from a talk by the French author Emmanuel Carrère. Carrère had spoken of the difficulty of depicting characters from the legendary past (in his case, the biblical figure of Saint Paul) as if they were human. He'd said that he took his guidance from early Renaissance paintings in which the multitude of faces in biblical scenes were obviously painted from life. That is, they were clearly portraits of specific people the painter had access to, including, sometimes, self-portraits. Carrère had explained that this had led him to believe that the verbal portrait of someone inaccessible to him would be possible to make only if he determined that it actually be a portrait of someone specific, not general—and that nearly anyone would do.

The story's writer has seized on this advice in an attempt to rescue his enterprise. If he wishes to avoid caricature or sentimentality in his depiction of the Native person who will intervene in his story, and teach the white family its deserved lesson, he must make that character a portrait of a specific human. He must avoid the generic figure of the benevolent trickster, or "magic Indian," who serves as the projected conscience in so many well-intentioned white narratives, from *One Flew Over the Cuckoo's Nest* to *Dead Man*. In this desire, he has landed, perhaps perversely, on recollection of an encounter of his own, with a man named Max Gros-Louis.

## Max Gros-Louis / "Telephone Line"

From Wikipedia:

> "Magella Gros-Louis OC [Order of Canada] OQ [Order
> of Quebec] (6 August 1931—14 November 2020), known
> as Max Gros-Louis or Oné Onti, was a Canadian politician
> and businessman in Quebec. For many years, he was Grand
> Chief of the Huron-Wendat First Nation. . . . Gros-Louis
> initially made a living by hunting, fishing and trapping. . . .
> He later opened a small shop "Le Huron" where he sold
> snowshoes, moccasins and other First Nation crafts, and also
> managed a dance company. In the course of his business he
> travelled widely to other indigenous communities and this
> led to his involvement in politics."

The story's writer met Max Gros-Louis when he was twelve years
old, on an anomalous family trip, with his mother and her boyfriend,
to Quebec, in midwinter. The boy had never previously been out of
the United States. His mother's boyfriend at the time was a younger
man, a New York City schoolteacher with a surprising amount of
money, perhaps from a family source, and he had swept the boy
and his siblings along on the impulsive voyage to French Canada.
What the boy remembers of the trip, aside from the encounter with
Max Gros-Louis, is French onion soup, buying a French version
of a *Spider–Man* comic book, morning croissants in the Château
Frontenac, and warming his frostbitten toes under the radiator at
that same hotel after a trudge through slush-crusted streets.

The story's writer had never met a Native tribal chief before, nor has he since. This is not a matter of avoidance but of happenstance. The story's writer came of age in the city, and has spent his life primarily in cities. He's known Native Americans! ("Some of my best friends are" etc.) The first were the elderly Mohawk women surviving in basement apartments in his childhood neighborhood, widows of the last of the men who built skyscrapers in Manhattan. (These skywalkers and their wives were also from French Canada, though he didn't know this at the time.) He met others, over time, though rarely those who'd been raised on tribal lands or who'd participated directly in tribal communities. In the life of his family, who were both hippies and Quakers, Native people were also symbolically charged, tragic emblems of some better and nobler existence. That this was a discourse that mixed much that was good with much that was bad, he'd understand later. But certainly it was affectionate, and intended to be respectful. The writer's father had copied out lines from *Black Elk Speaks* into his high school graduation book, for instance. Another example: as a child he'd practically memorized an LP by a Native folk singer named Floyd Westerman, called *Custer Died for Your Sins*. Some of the writer's midwestern relatives liked to claim a small portion of their lineage as Native. That this was a common fantasy he'd also understand later.

His encounter with Max Gros-Louis, though, was a singular one. The writer's mother and her boyfriend had sought it out, a variation in their Quebec tourism, the majority of which had been in pursuit of the fantasy that they'd actually traveled to

Paris (croissants, onion soup, etc.). They'd gone to where the city met the reservation to find Gros-Louis's business, a shop called Centre d'Artisanat Le Huron. They'd encouraged the boy to speak with Gros-Louis—to meet the chief, who'd dressed for his role in fringed leather and a headband. The boy had come away with the impression of someone kind, formidable, and quite tall—but also of someone with some tightly held feeling of amused tolerance of those who'd come to meet him.

The boy and his family didn't buy much, as he recalls it. No moccasins, no headdress, no artwork. Likely in this they represented a disappointment. The boy, however, did purchase a postcard. He was a postcard collector in those days.

It is when the boy becomes the story's writer, nearly fifty years later, that he recognizes that in a semi-conscious way he has always associated Max Gros-Louis with the figure in Lafferty's story, Clarence Little-Saddle, the recipient and rebuffer of the white family's attempt to occupy the narrow valley. It is also only when the story's writer conceives this attempt to rewrite Lafferty, and connects this to his memory of Gros-Louis, that he troubles to Google "Max Gros-Louis" and discovers, from his obituaries, that he was alive until 2020, that he was elected to serve as the grand chief of the Huron-Wendat Nation in three separate periods across five decades, and that he was regarded as one of the truly great leaders in the First Nations cause in Canada's history.

Had the story's writer imagined that Gros-Louis was some kind of trickster or charlatan, a pretend chief who was really a seller of tourist merchandise? No. Yet in his astonishment at what he learns from the obituaries, the story's writer realizes he had imagined that Gros-Louis was frozen in time as he was in the encounter's recollection—that he was a kind of private dream nudging at the writer's awareness. In this, the writer is too typical of himself. That the past lives in him, and stirs him, doesn't mean that the past lives inside of himself. The past too is a narrow valley, one refusing occupation. Or no. That's wrong. The past is huge, and real, but you are small. To reenter the valley of the past is, properly, to grow tiny, and to vanish.

## What about the Winnebago? / "Mr. Blue Sky" (reprise)

The Winnebago believes it is moving, but it is parked. The family believes they are outside, rumbling steadily west across the landscape, in pursuit of the valley, the open space, the tabula rasa, but they are mistaken. Such beliefs are belated, lapsed, overdue, like a book once checked out from a library and then lost for decades; the story has moved indoors, the frontier has become one of recursion, quotation, paraphrase, allegory. To be specific, the frontier is now an "electronic frontier." The Winnebago is parked in front of a casino, deep in a tribal nation's territory. The family is shrunken, though they do not suffer from the dysmorphia that accompanies their shrinking; they remain unaware of their tininess, their insignificance. The family are together playing a gambling game that is a video game, designed to separate them from their money. The game is called Win-and-They-Go! The action consists of attempting to place homesteads on every hundred acres of open territory, a frantic effort destined, as in all gambling devices, to tease and entice with sporadic success and to bring only eventual total failure and defeat. The soundtrack of the game consists of songs licensed from the band ELO; the design of the "frontier," which repeats like the backdrop in a *Flintstones* cartoon, across which the family navigates, consists of cacti, distant canyon bluffs, abandoned gold mines, wood-paneled station wagons, and crafty winking trickster Indians selling merchandise at trading posts. All of this is rendered in a nostalgic 1970s-cartoon style, but the story, it is now apparent, takes place not in 1979, but in the present. The past, even so recent a past as 1979, a time in which a paraphrase of Lafferty's story could still properly be written, is unsustainable. The machine is sucking money from the family's coffers. It's OK, they have a lot of it. The story dollies out, now, to leave the family there, in the windowless bowels of the casino, to rise up and note the Winnebago in the parking lot, amid so many other unwieldy vacation vehicles also stilled there. The story climbs ever higher to a wide pan of the surrounding desert, then higher, to find the horizon. The story acknowledges its collapse at this vanishing point, not a frontier of any type or variety. The story acknowledges its relief at being over even as it acknowledges the possibility that it never managed to begin. Game over. Thanks for playing.

# "Rooms Full of Old Books Are Immortal Enough for Me"

Jonathan Lethem interviewed by Terry Bisson

*What was it like to get the MacArthur "genius" award? What did it do for you?*

I was in Maine when I got that news. The fateful call. A peninsula neighbor also got one that year, a guy studying lobster fishing science, crustacean reproductive patterns under climate change and so forth. A big hero to the lobster-dependent community. The next day the local newspaper, the *Ellsworth American*, had an above-the-fold story, "Area Man Wins Genius Award." It wasn't me they meant. That was good perspective.

A joke that I'm stealing from Colson Whitehead: It's much like being Charly from "Flowers for Algernon." You peak for a year or two, and then you go back to being an ordinary person. It's a long time ago, and it's generous of you to recall I was briefly a genius—which, by the way, is a word the MacArthur people are always trying to deny but that attaches itself to their fellowships in a persistent folkloric way.

Another joke, which is my own, is that they don't send you special MacArthur money that comes in a special MacArthur wallet and which you can only spend on esoteric genius things. I paid off a couple of people's college loans, got my credit card out of the red, took a pleasure trip to New Zealand, and then lived on the residue for a few years instead of teaching. That's to say, it was rent, food, and health care. The direct results were *Chronic City* and the essay "The Ecstasy of Influence," two of the better things I ever managed, in my own opinion.

*You seem to periodically but somewhat dependably come back to detective and science fiction. Is this a salute or homage to genre roots, or is something more devious or serious at work?*

I'm relieved you notice. Sometimes I see people breaking me into two halves, as if after *The Fortress of Solitude* I became somebody other than myself. It feels sad to see this; it suggests that those making that division are utterly incurious about the books that followed, which include a surreal apocalypse with space travel, a gothic horror novel with ESP, a detective novel with ecological themes, and a postcollapse pastoral. Not to show ingratitude to your generous question, but I'd even quibble with "roots" and certainly with "salute or homage," as if I'm off to one side, tipping my cap to these things that in fact nourish and constitute me. The work is fed by many roots, almost all located in the voracious reading of my teenage years and early twenties. This list won't be exhaustive, and I've dropped these names before, but Delany, Kafka, Dick, Greene, Highsmith, Kavan, L. Carroll, Le Guin, Chandler, C. Stead, Willeford, Baldwin, Murdoch, Borges, Lem, Ballard, DeLillo. My books are the *branches*. From the inside, my writing feels like one continuous exploration, not a sequence of tactics. The differences are in publishing context and in the reception, not what I'm doing when I sit down. This all sounds immodest as can be, so I should add that I'm fully aware that it's a ridiculous privilege to be able to speak of having a "reception." Compared to most artists of any kind, I've been showered with attention. I'm absurdly lucky.

*You inherited the chair at Pomona College once held by the late David Foster Wallace. Did you ever know or meet him?*

By weird chance one of my childhood friends from Brooklyn went to Amherst and knew him, so during our respective college years I was told, "There's this guy in my dorm who's a writer too and he's really smart and you guys are interested in similar things and you should meet him." Then he became DFW and I became a bookstore clerk. Some kids I knew in college were also publishing books years before I could even place a short story in a magazine. Later on, he and I knew some people in common, so I always imagined we'd say hello at some point and I could tell him the Amherst story, but no.

*What is Creative Writing at Pomona? Who takes it and why? What do you provide?*

Pomona's an undergraduate college, so I'm not teaching MFA students, as so many novelists end up doing. Instead, we're in the realm of a liberal arts education, with creative writing as a feature of the "humanities." I'm enclosed in a highly varied English department, and if you work with me a lot, the most that can produce is a college diploma as an English major. This takes a lot of pressure off, happily. We're not a professional finishing school for either authors or creative writing instructors; we're studying literature and daring to try to think about it and try to make some at the same time. That's to say, it's a good conversation that involves a lot of reading. I think of myself as a teacher of reading, really, apart from providing a few tips on where the quote marks usually go in a paragraph that includes dialogue, and why you probably shouldn't let your characters gaze into mirrors and describe themselves at length. I teach the kind of reading that encompasses reading your own drafts and the drafts of others, but also examples of published work ranging from canonical things to the work of young writers who might be just a few years or months out ahead of your own aspirations. It's fun.

*Your nonfiction is often as personal as your fiction or even more. Does the apparatus of fiction (plot, POV, etc.) propel or constrain you?*
That's interesting. I suspect you're right. I don't find anything constraining in fiction, so it may be that when I'm romping in that infinite playground, I forget to find "myself" directly interesting. There are so many other things to focus on. Anyway, "myself" will usually crop up uninvited, so I don't have to worry about it. By contrast, in my essays I trip up on notions of authority or subjectivity or positionality—the problem of who-the-hell-is-it-who-is-having-these-opinions? So I begin reflecting on my own person as a form of preliminary grounding, for the reader and myself. And then I wander into reminiscence and end up writing a confessional essay as much as opining on the matter at hand.

*Do you write as a job or when the muse strikes you? Any particular routine?*

I like everything better when I'm writing—myself, the sunrise, the sunset, food. I don't mean writing incessantly, just routinely. Usually two or three hours is the maximum, and sometimes it's a lot less. I like being regularly attached to a project that excites me and returning to it most days, if not every day, to make contact with my own thinking, to extend the notions a bit further, to refine some sentences I wrote the day or week before to make them clearer or funnier or to produce more meaning than they managed the first time. It's been life-habit for so long that I think of it as more or less consonant with being alive—to be writing something. I can no longer imagine being without it, though of course I know I might be robbed of it, as one can contemplate being robbed of a sense or a limb.

The routine? Mornings are good. They don't have to be early. Just whenever you get up, after the coffee, get to the desk. It's morning right now.

*Your essay on plagiarism, "The Ecstasy of Influence," was (to me) as rightly contrarian as T.S. Eliot's "Tradition and the Individual Talent." Did you pitch that to* Harper's *or was it their idea?*

I sat in a restaurant and pitched it to an editor named Luke Mitchell, who has pulled out of me several of my best and most-committed essays over the years. Then came almost two years of work; it was the dissertation I thought I'd never have to write when I dropped out of college.

*When you dropped out of college in your sophomore year, you hit the road. I did the same. Seems a sophomore thing. What did you know about Berkeley that drew you, or did you just end up there?*

I threw myself at Berkeley, as if at a dartboard, when I needed to be distant from the East Coast. I think the Bay Area destination carried a faint residue of a Beat Generation script that had gotten into my head—a whiff of countercultural freedom, the Free Speech Movement, et cetera. It was the copious used bookstores that kept me there for ten years—and the friends and lovers I met on the staffs of used bookstores.

*Your* Jeopardy *question: I provide the answer, you provide the question. Answer: Heaven without immortality.*

See above. I don't believe in immortality, but the used bookstores that are my heaven are going to outlive me, and that feels good. When the writer Richard Price was asked whether The Novel was dead, he said, "The Novel will be at your funeral." Rooms full of old books are immortal enough for me.

*Is Plot for you a mentor, a taskmaster, or a companion?*

I tell my students that I think plot is a chimera. There's often talk of it as if it can be identified, or intentionally produced, but I think plot is more a term of praise, one that pretends it is a quantifiable thing: "I loved the plot!" What you can identify, and design, happens not on some overall "plot" level, but locally, page by page. Things like implication, velocity, and causality and surprise. Occurrences tumbling out of other occurrences, and piling up with a pleasing sense of implication and possibility, and in unexpected ways, and at an agreeable rate. You can't really talk about plot the way you can point to the composition in a painting or the melody in a song. It's just what it feels like when that other good stuff accumulates.

*Fairly early in your career, you showed up at some of the Famous Writer shows, Yaddo and suchlike. What put you on their radar? Was that a thrill?*

I sought it all out, promiscuously, as guided by my reading, and by my teenage fascination with the lives of authors. I wanted to be a Yaddo guest, and a guest of honor at an SF convention, and to visit foreign cities where I would sit on panels where we needed interpreters to understand one another, and to see my books put into weird leatherbound volumes, and to publish in underground zines and the *New Yorker*. I wanted to guest-edit "Year's Best" anthologies and help revive lost authors and write introductions to G.K. Chesterton and Anna Kavan and Walter Tevis; I wanted to interview musicians for *Rolling Stone*; I wanted to blurb books and judge prizes and collaborate with other writers; I wanted to write a Marvel comic book; I wanted to do one of the most obscure things an author can do, I think: finish a book another writer had left unfinished when they died. I did that with Don Carpenter. I did *all* of those things, which made me silly with joy even when it was boring. But most of those things only have to happen once. The simpler acts of reading and writing are what I want to do all the time.

*Do you still collect books? Vinyl records?*

I never quit accumulating books, and some of the pursuits within that accumulation are specific enough to call "collecting." For instance, I'm trying to put together a run of the first hundred Ace Doubles—I currently have twenty-six of the hundred, including an "Ace-1," which I can't help bragging about. I love books so much I am forced also to love cardboard boxes and barns and attics and storage spaces— I'm headed over to one of the storage spaces after I finish writing this morning, only I'm afraid I can't remember the combination of the lock. I started accumulating vinyl records again after a two-decade pause where I accumulated CDs and MP3s instead. But none of these things go away—I still listen to the CDs and MP3s and the vinyl.

*The poem seems one of the few literary forms you have not tried, at least onstage. How come? What poets do you read for fun?*

What are you, a mind reader? I was just wanting to tell you about my first-ever poetry collection, *Horse with No Cake: Selected Poems and Lyrics*, which is about to come out from Another Sun Press. Buy it on their website. It only took me forty years to accumulate enough of the things for a 120-page volume—and half of that is song lyrics, from my collaborations with musicians. Every single one of them was written in rueful appreciation of how difficult it is, what a remarkable form of disciplined attention, to center one's writing self in poetic work continuously, or even on a regular basis. It's beyond me. Instead, these things were mostly written to occasions, as gifts or asides, or in assumed voices. Still, I'm proud that the book exists. I won't live long enough to follow it up.

My favorite poets to read when, as a teenager, I briefly believed I might really be a poet, were the New York school and some of their relations: Kenneth Koch, John Ashbery, James Schuyler, Eileen Myles, Ron Padgett. I also read Surrealist and Dada poetry because I was into everything Surrealist, the collages and paintings and films and feuds. Then in the Bay Area I fell in with some poets: Steve Benson, Ron Silliman, Gloria Frym, Owen Hill, Tom Clark, others. I like the company of poets the way I like the company of painters, and I read my friends.

*Does your car have a pet name? I hope not.*
A story: The first car I owned entirely on my own—a New York kid, I was a late driver—was a Toyota Corolla gifted to me by an ex's pitying parents. All the silver paint was scuffed off to reveal a dull matte metal color. It was pretty run down. I got a vanity license plate reading SQUALOR. (My friend Angus MacDonald had a vanity plate that said RADIO ON, from the Modern Lovers song— the best vanity plate I think I'll ever see.) I drove SQUALOR around Berkeley and Oakland for three or four years. Once the cartoonist Daniel Clowes invited me to his home, and when I drove up in SQUALOR he exclaimed, "That's your car? I love that car!" Later on, my sister drove SQUALOR, which turned out to be an indomitable car, and then she gave it away, and someone used it as the getaway car in the robbery of a Carl's Jr. True story.

*John Crowley once told me that the secret subtext of his work is always: this is a book. Well, okay. So, what's the secret subtext of yours?*

Isn't Crowley's the subtext of *every* book? I'm always so envious of other writers' answers to these aphoristic questions. Like for instance, "Why do you write?," to which Thomas Berger said, "Because it isn't there," and Bernard Malamud said, "I would be too moved to say," each of which seems too perfect to hope to match. Maybe the subtext of my books is "Wouldn't it be interesting to be someone else? How can I best approximate it?" Maybe that isn't even the subtext, just the text.

*What's the deal with the jukebox on your website? Are you trying to hitch a ride on rock?*

Is rock going somewhere? It looks to me like it just sits there. I'll keep an eye on it in case you're right.

Seriously, the sequence of collaborations with musicians has been one of the most unlikely pleasures of writing life.

*Were you surprised when Dylan won the Nobel Prize? Are you still?*

The morning after the announcement, before I heard any reaction, I happened to be listening to Claudia Rankine talk live on the *Brian Lehrer Show* on WNYC. She'd been booked, obviously, before the Dylan Nobel thing and just happened to be a poet on the radio the morning the news dropped. Lehrer asked her what she thought, and Rankine said, "His words are in all our mouths." Holding on to this simple acknowledgement of what seems an obvious truth—that he changed the language—was useful to me once all the debate started about what constitutes literature. I get that it bugs people because he could be seen as not needing the thing any more than he needed his Oscar, and there are writers on whom the award would have shone a spotlight. Maybe there should be more prizes, or fewer. I don't know.

*The Arrest is set on a little Maine peninsula occupied by out-of-the-way, oddball types. Is there actually such a place?*
Yes and no—but you knew that would be my answer, right? I'm "there" now, enjoying the sight of some wild turkeys walking past the window facing my desk. Here at the start of summer I've been being an oddball with my oddball friends for the past week—swimming in the ocean, playing pétanque, eating fish that my friend Sergei caught, moving books in and out of storage spaces, and dreaming of opening a used bookstore so I can hang out there with whoever walks in. I'm grateful this place exists. Then again, *The Arrest* is fundamentally an allegorical space, a rubber reality, projected into existence by the fictional notions that occupy it. A cartoon, if the word doesn't seem too much a demurral from serious intent. Most of my books are serious cartoons, set in places that may share names with real ones, or not, but which are only obliquely depictions of those places, and serve mainly as a proscenium for my clowns and tragedians. So, no. Tinderwick, from *The Arrest*, isn't here, it's *here*—assuming you can see me right now, pointing my forefinger at my forehead.

I believe this is my baseline mode. It defines my short stories, and each of my first five novels (up to and including *Motherless Brooklyn*). The exceptions are three longer books about outerborough New York City. First *Fortress of Solitude*, where I began to do some social history work—tentatively. I was trained as a visual artist and was a failure as a student otherwise, so my capacity for study and research was a muscle that developed slowly. In *Dissident Gardens* I got a bit more deliberate about it. That's fiction as social history. And the book I'm writing now goes there again. But *The Arrest* makes no claim as an authoritative depiction of Maine or the towns on this peninsula. Its seriousness is as a conjuration.

*Ever been down the Gowanus Canal in a canoe? I have.*
I'm no fan of black mayonnaise, which is how the toxic chemical gunk at the bottom of the Gowanus has been described. Canoes tip. I might tackle it in a diving bell.

*Were you in New York on 9/11?*
I was. I wrote about it directly for a couple of magazines but couldn't get the feeling on the page to any real satisfaction. I shouldn't have included those pieces in *The Ecstasy of Influence* collection. I did better when I treated it askew, under other names, in *Chronic City*. I began writing that in 2006, at which point I was able to see the experience less in isolation, more as a crescendo of intricate historical nightmares—stuff extending on invisible strings beyond the moment itself.

*Ever miss Brooklyn? (My wife asked me to ask you.)*
Missing Brooklyn is so deep and basic to me that, when I'm there, I miss missing it.

# My Year of Reading Lemmishly

JUNE 1978. A BOY and his grandmother have traveled on the A train to the New York Coliseum, a convention center at Columbus Circle. She was a trustee of the Queensboro Public Library, with comp tickets that will get them into the American Library Association's national conference; he was a fifteen-year-old book fetishist and stone science fiction fan.

The convention hall's exhibition booths featured, along with lots of plastic slipcovers and display racks, tables full of books from those publishers who specifically relied upon library sales for their viability. That's to say, a lot of reference books, a lot of specialty nonfiction, and a dearth of science fiction. But the kid's antennae were good. At the booth of the Seabury Press (a publishing division of the Episcopalian Church) he spotted four anomalous hardcovers, all by an author with a peculiar name. *Memoirs Found in a Bathtub*, *The Futurological Congress*, *The Invincible*, and *The Cyberiad*. Two—*Invincible* and *Memoirs*—sported cover art easily recognizable as "SF art." Their jackets were designed by Richard Powers, whose unmistakable paintings were usually featured on Ballantine mass-market paperbacks by Isaac Asimov, Frederic Pohl, Clifford Simak, and others. Powers's designs resembled surrealist paintings, specifically those of Yves Tanguy and Max Ernst. They screamed of the "paraliterary": of druggy, trippy sci-fi—just the boy's cup of tea. The other two dust jackets—on *The Futurological Congress* and *The Cyberiad*—were more restrained, looking like prestigious European art-house fiction. *Congress* featured a drawing by Paul Klee. It was as though Seabury, wavering as to what sort of writer they'd acquired, nervously split the difference. The boy wasn't fooled: the crazy titles of the two books with "tasteful" covers were enticing enough.

"Will you buy me these?"

His grandmother scowled. She was, at times, a tough customer. It was not enough that the boy be bookish: he should be the right kind of bookish. What the hell were these? What was a Lem? "All four?"

"Yes, please."

Skeptically, with an arched eyebrow, the grandmother purchased the display copies. This made it a life-changing day in the life of the boy. I write this with those four Seabury hardcovers on the desk beside me.

Shouldn't I be just the person for a centenary piece on Stanisław Lem? *Novelist and philosopher of technology, author of* Solaris *and scores of novels, stories, and essays, one of the great figures in Polish literature, the greatest non-English-language science fiction writer between Jules Verne and Cixin Liu, born a hundred years ago . . .* The trouble, beyond the fact that I've dawdled past that anniversary, is, well, everything. All the unstated premises, all the undefined terms (especially "science fiction"). As my grandmother would put it, I know bupkis about Polish literature, aside from the greatness of Olga Tokarczuk (one of whose blurbs reads: "I have read Lem all my life. . . . He freed my imagination . . .") and that the title of Lem's novel *Memoirs Found in a Bathtub* makes reference to Jan Potocki's *The Manuscript Found in Saragossa*.

The centenary train is leaving the station. Poland's parliament declared 2021 the "Year of Lem," while publishers have launched the "Lem 100" project—one hundred books worldwide, with the centenary imprint. *Solaris* can be purchased in at least twenty languages with George Clooney's face on the jacket (the wrong filmed rendition). In the US, the MIT press has inaugurated a reprint series with new introductions commissioned from eminences in the fields of science fiction and technology. Having, like Tokarczuk, read Lem all my life—or, more precisely, boasted all my life of having read Lem, since I actually gobbled the books in a mad spate in my youth—I should jump aboard. First, I told myself, I'd read or reread "all of Lem."

#

I couldn't. Lem's first, non-SF novel, *The Hospital of the Transfiguration*, written in the late 1940s, and depicting a young doctor's wartime internship in a psychiatric hospital, was translated in 1988. But Lem's earliest SF novels, *Man from Mars* and *The Astronauts*, weren't. He dismissed these as mutilated by a subservience to Soviet ideology. Hence his career in English begins with two novels published in Poland in 1959.* His turn to science fiction was in the spirit of other Iron Curtain artists who slipped below the censor's radar in forms regarded as unserious, like animated film. Further books from Lem's later period, and innumerable essays, remain untranslated. I couldn't read *On Site Inspection*, or *Provocation*, or *Darkness and Mildew*—such tantalizing titles!—unless I learned Polish.†

As a teenager I was oblivious to the matter of translation. I've come around. My sister and my partner are both literary translators; my first editor was Stanisław Lem's translator. At some point I'd learned that *Solaris* itself hadn't been translated into English directly, but from a Polish-to-French translation, with a result Lem described as "drastic"—a beautiful, bitter irony for a book that takes as its subject the impossibility of meaningful contact between alien species. Perhaps I should wonder: had I ever read Lem at all?

Anyhow, Lem was incommensurable—to SF, to literature, to himself. He was so many different writers—five, at least. I had too much to read. I risked missing the centenary in mute tribute, lost within the literary hyperobject that was Lem.

---

* Though one of the two, *Eden*, wasn't published in the United States until 1989. Like many writers in translation, Lem's chronology in translation was reshuffled incoherently.

† My bibliography depends on the work of prolific Canadian literary and media critic Peter Swirski, author of at least four or five books on Lem, and reader and translator of Polish. Swirski ought to be writing this piece.

#

Could I at least name the five Lems? The first is the author of *Eden* (1959), *Solaris* (1961), *Return from the Stars* (1961), *Fiasco* (1986), and innumerable short stories about an interstellar navigator named Pirx. That's to say, a twentieth-century "hard SF" writer, one of both visionary gifts and an inexhaustible diligence at the task of "extrapolation."

Hard SF is that tradition originating less in Mary Shelley's gothic *Frankenstein* than with H.G. Wells's technological prognostications. The hard SF tradition likes Jules Verne, the predictor of submarines and holograms, but frowns at his fanciful plots. Standardized in the midcentury US, under John W. Campbell Jr.'s editorship of *Astounding* magazine, hard SF advertises consumer goods like personal robots and flying cars. It valorizes space travel culminating in successful (if difficult) contact with the alien life assumed to be widely strewn throughout the galaxies, and glows with a self-ratifying "Sense of Wonder." This movement, exemplified by names like Heinlein, Asimov, and Clarke, SF's sturdy dead-white-guy canon, is where the fascination with technology and the future went to get mashed up with American exceptionalist ideology: technocratic triumphalism, Manifest Destiny, Libertarian survivalist bullshit. Hard SF fueled both the Cold War–era space race and, soon after, Ronald Reagan's "Star Wars" dream. As Adam Curtis showed in the BBC series *Pandora's Box*, the notion of defensive missiles in space was essentially whispered into the cowboy actor's ear by two leading conservative hard-SF writers of the '80s, Larry Niven and Jerry Pournelle.

"Extrapolation" may be a purer ideal. The term is an import from the realm of mathematics: a writer, keenly observing the world around them, can measure its trends and implications, then offer persuasive suppositions about what comes next. Yet, like "multitasking" or "Tantric sex," extrapolation is a thing easier to name than to find examples of very many people really doing, or doing well. A few, like Philip K. Dick, seem cursed to it as an abreactive symptom, a cry of protest at living through the twentieth century. Lem belongs in that company of SF writers—Wells, Olaf Stapledon, Kim Stanley Robinson, a few others—who practiced intentional extrapolation with regular and sustained success.

Is prescience the measure of SF as an art? An attractive truism says that the best writing about the future isn't, really, but rather is a lens for apprehending the present: Orwell's *Nineteen Eighty-Four* is an allegorical X-ray of 1948, and so forth. Lem himself, in an interview, points out that Kafka's "In the Penal Colony" isn't better than *The Castle* for having come true. (The example he chooses is typically dire.) Then again, perhaps these two things are really one: to actually bring oneself to see the present *is* to see the future. Lem—as he was never above bragging—was a ridiculously good predictor.

Lem One resembles a hard SF writer not only in this extrapolative sense, but in his consuming fascination with space travel and the idea of "first contact," and in his valorization of the figures of astronaut, inventor, explorer: worlds of bravery and sacrifice, of masculinity. Lem's spaceships are as devoid of women as Melville's whaling ships; the important exception, *Solaris*, offers a "human" woman conjured for the protagonist by an alien intelligence. Lem shares hard SF's bottomless appetite for scrupulous descriptions of imaginary landscapes and nonexistent machines, and its intoxication with dwarfing scale: light years, eons, quadrillions.

#

Lem also wrote mock fairy tales and folk tales of the future, phantasmagorical satires, Kafkaesque allegories of twentieth-century alienation, and stories of horror of the cosmic or existential variety, evoking Poe and Lovecraft.‡ Call him Lem Two. His many books include *The Cyberiad*, a cycle of techno-fables which many, including Kim Stanley Robinson and Lem's most crucial English translator, Michael Kandel, claim as their favorite, and the paranoidpicaresque novels *Memoirs Found in a Bathtub* and *The Futurological Congress*, which as a teenage reader I made my talismans.

The preoccupations of Lem Two resemble those of Lem One. The iconography: robots, scientists, inventors, space travel, impossible aliens. There's even a funhouse mirror version of Pirx the Pilot, a droll and resilient voyager through absurdist futures named Ijon Tichy. Like Pirx, Tichy features in enough short stories to fill two collections; both characters hang around long enough to play the protagonists in Lem's final two full-length novels. Lem Two's themes are similar as well. Loosely, these are the inadequacy

---

‡    Lem Two is perhaps the largest and most various in my compendium, and could probably be broken down further into sub-Lems, but enough is enough.

of our species' collective intelligence in the face of our irrational animal natures; in the face of our own proliferating and increasingly autonomous inventions; and in the face of a genuinely alien Other. In Lem's view, faced with this triple threat, we slump into the defensive use of reductive ideologies and superstitions, into anthropomorphic projection and solipsistic withdrawal, and, ultimately, into nihilism, cruelty, and nervous breakdown.

In another sense, the second Lem is the first's opposite. The first exalts realistic science, regards the future seriously as a destination our species will have to endure, and sneers at fantasy and exaggeration; the second makes every and any SF gesture fodder for metaphor, allegory, and surrealist "defamiliarization," while mixing spaceships and aliens freely with kings and queens, dragons and monsters. The second Lem sometimes resembles the Italo Calvino of *t zero* and *Cosmicomics*, in whom SF riffs are completely subsumed in metaphor. Elsewhere, Lem Two seems to glance back to Swift, Voltaire, and Gogol, or sideways to Borges and Pynchon. These are the kinds of names the SF tradition has often claimed, to decorate their wrong-side-of-the-tracks clubhouse. Yet those writers would be bewildered at the clannish rituals and arcane litmus tests typical of the genre.

But before I probe Lem's relationship with the culture of Western SF—a marvelously scurrilous topic—I should detail the three Lems trailing along after Lem One and Lem Two.

#

Lem Three wrote just two novels, yet he could easily be, on the right day, one's favorite. *The Investigation* (1959) and *The Chain of Chance* (1976) are a matched set of ontological whodunnits, both centered on mysterious sequences of crimes whose only plausible suspects appear to be the universe itself. Their cases resolve divergently (I'm avoiding spoilers) but together form a rebuke to generic expectation, a dialectic on our urge to frame and solve mysteries in the first place.

*The Investigation*, written by a brilliant young man who'd perhaps never yet left Poland, is set in England, in a wheezy and secondhand Scotland Yard milieu, and reads like a conscious throwback to Conan Doyle and G.K. Chesterton. The air of paradox aligns the book with morbid philosophical spoofs like Gerald Kersh's *Prelude to a Certain Midnight*, and anticipates Paul Auster.

*Chain of Chance*, written fifteen years later by a worldly author who had achieved success in the West and had moved his residence to Vienna, is Lem's best pass at a "contemporary" novel of the '70s. Its modish air of European terrorism and ennui evokes Godard or Antonioni films, or DeLillo books like *Players* or *Running Dog*. It was praised in the *New Yorker* by John Updike, who noted that Lem's "sanguine temperament" mellowed the "cruel mathematics" of his worldview. Updike singled out one hallucinatory sequence where the investigator is psychotropically poisoned: "Only a mind habituated to seeing the human mind from the outside, as a chemical and electrical machine, could evoke derangement with such cool clarity."§ For these two books alone, for their remorseless re-working of what human "investigation" might consist of, Lem could be remembered.

#

Lem Four is the pure postmodernist, who unified his essayistic and fictional selves with an openly Borgesian or Nabokovian gesture. *A Perfect Vacuum* (1971), *Imaginary Magnitude* (1973), and *One Human Minute* (1983) consist entirely of reviews and forewords to nonexistent books. Most of these are scientific treatises full of mis-anthropic fulmination, with titles like "The World as Cataclysm" and "Civilization as a Mistake" and "On the Impossibility of Life." One, "A Perfect Vacuum," reviews the book in which it appears. These satirical miniatures perfectly somersault over every trap. The reader benefits from Lem's obvious delight and relief at dispensing with fiction's theatrical mechanics, which had begun to irritate him. What's left is the ventriloquized voice of the scholars and

---

§    Updike, who reviewed the book in tandem with Barbara Pym's *Excellent Women*, took the opportunity to complain that neither author provided much in the way of sex appeal—in verse:

Pym and Lem
Lem and Pym—
There's little love
In her or him.
Out on a limb
With Pym and Lem
One hugs oneself
Instead of them.

A glimpse of a different New Yorker, and a different world.

autodidacts who've written the imaginary books, Lem's Kinbotes and Pierre Menards. Lem Four is a kind of magic act.

#

Lem Five? He's another major figure: the prolific essayist, futurist, and literary critic. Lem's pronouncements on technology and culture range copiously and burrow deeply. A supreme armchair anythingist, Lem is magisterial. He shows no hesitation in dismissing Hegel ("a complete idiot"), *Gravity's Rainbow* ("an utterly demented dud"), or Buddhism ("the terrifying anachronism of their teachings and instructions").

Lem's *Summa Technologiae*, a torrential magnum opus of futurism and speculative philosophy, written in his miraculous years of 1961 to 1964, was finally published in English by the University of Minnesota Press in 2013. Sections like "Prolegomena to Omnipotence" and "A Lampoon of Evolution," and chapters headed "The Dangers of Electocracy" and "Cyborgization" announce a cascade of insights and speculations. The book manages to anticipate or preempt, among others, Donna Haraway, Richard Dawkins, Timothy Morton, and whole shelves of cyberpunk fiction and object-oriented ontology. Lem should have been recognized as a great futurologist, though the book's density and dry wit would never have sold like Buckminster Fuller or Alvin Toffler. He could also be seen as one of the founders of media studies. Proud and anxious at what he'd achieved, Lem would find himself demoralized by the book's lack of reach, and at the paucity of translations. He revised and expanded *Summa* for a decade, then defended its prognostications in "Twenty Years After" and "Thirty Years After." He wouldn't live to see it done in English.

Lem-the-seer is exasperated, eccentrically lyrical and permanently fresh. One only has to dip into the chapter called "Phantomatics" to see that in 1964 Lem already grasped more of the implications of virtual reality—of "Meta"—than Mark Zuckerberg ever will. On the one hand, the inadequacies of the imagination of the VR user ensure that one is destined to be patronized and infantilized by one's own devices:

> Put briefly, the more the character one wishes to impersonate differs in personality traits and historical period from his own, the more fictitious, naïve, or even primitive his behavior and the whole vision will be. Because, to be crowned a king or receive the Pope's emissaries, one has to be familiar with the whole court protocol. The persons created by the phantomat can pretend that they cannot see the idiotic behavior of the ermine-clad national bank clerk, and thus his own pleasure will perhaps not diminish as a result of his mistakes, but we can clearly see that this whole situation is steeped in triviality and buffoonery. This is why it will be very hard for phantomatics to develop into a mature dramatic form.

Conversely, the feedback loop created by machines that have been programmed to grow better and better at fooling you will rapidly spiral into narcissistic breakdown:

Psychiatrists would still see various neurotics in their waiting rooms, haunted by obsessions of a new type—the fear that what they are experiencing is not true at all and that they have become "trapped" in a "phantomatic world." I mention this point because it clearly indicates how technology not only shapes normal consciousness but also makes its way onto the list of diseases and disorders whose emergence it initiates.

Lem goes on to speculate that the endgame, as the illusion-matrix perfects itself, might force users into a logical trap in which the only person they could trust for authentication would be themselves, since any given friend—or lover, or psychiatrist—could actually be a seamlessly rendered product of the phantomat, and therefore under the guidance of one's enemy (or, more banally, they might be simply an advertisement for something). In fact, this neatly allegorizes the condition of social media already, even before one puts on the goggles and gloves. What is sometimes called "siloing" may be cultivating a vast collective experience of paranoid-solipsism, a suspicion of the inauthenticity of anyone but ourselves. We imagine we wander free from it when we step back from our screens, yet its code has rewritten the outer reality.

The other place the nonfiction Lem is on view in English is in *Microworlds* (1984), a collection of literary essays, including those that got Lem kicked out of the Science Fiction Writers of America, the genre's trade union. It featured essays praising Borges, Gogol, and Kafka, alongside snapshots of his disappointment with

American SF. The disappointment—his disdain—was vast. It was planetary. Two of the book's essays are titled "Science Fiction: A Hopeless Case, with Exceptions" and "Philip K. Dick: A Visionary among the Charlatans." When these, along with another essay, not collected in the book, with the even more blunt title "Looking Down on Science Fiction: A Novelist's Choice for the World's Worst Writing," were circulated among SFWA members, the resultant tempest was revealing, on both sides.

#

From my teens well into my twenties, the period when my notion of myself as a writer was under construction (which isn't to say that it may not still be) I identified strongly—too strongly?—with Stanisław Lem. Lems One through Four had blown my mind (I hadn't encountered Five), and that they were all one writer had inspired my hope that I too could vary wildly, that I could straddle modes and worlds. I liked his name, and that my own could be anagrammed to 'The Lem'; I liked that I'd be near him on the bookshelves (we'd be in sequence with Le Guin and Lessing, also crucial to me)—if only I could get published. When my first novel was finally picked up, its editor was none other than Michael Kandel, who when my agent began to explain Kandel's somewhat marginal status as the editor of a nonexistent SF program at Harcourt, Brace & Jovanovich I interrupted to say, "That's Stanisław Lem's translator!"❡ The science fiction page in the HBJ

---

❡   I shouldn't allow my special affection—or Lem's—for Kandel,

catalogue that featured my book had only two other authors on it: Lem and Italo Calvino. Kandel told me stories of how Lem liked to zip around Vienna in his lemon-yellow sports car. Heaven.

Once I was on my way, I plundered a hallucinatory set-piece from *The Futurological Congress* to make a hallucinatory set-piece for my third novel, *As She Climbed across the Table*. And I mentioned Lem constantly. He was part of a litany for me, the "International Fabulators," I'd recite at the drop of a hat: Julio Cortázar, Italo Calvino, Kobo Abe, Angela Carter, Stanisław Lem (and behind them the inescapable Kafka and Borges). These weren't the only writers I admired, or aped. But I thought that invocation of their names, in particular, legitimated the kinds of things *I* was trying to do. How pretentious.

The limits of this identification were obvious. I lacked Lem's sheer cognition, obviously. Lem came from Polish physicians; I

---

to suggest that I'm unaware that I owe my access to Lem's texts to the efforts of a veritable army of translators, new and old: Joel Stern, Maria Swiecicka-Ziemianek, Christine Rose, Adele Milch, William Brand, Marc Heine, Louis Iribarne, Magdelena Majcherczyk, Elinor Ford, Catherine Leach, Joanna Zylinska, Bill Johnston, Antonia Lloyd-Jones, and others I fear I may have missed. What authority I lack in praising their efforts, by not knowing the Polish originals, may be partly made up by the extent of my immersion: I recognize Lem when I hear his voice, and I do. As for Wendayne Ackerman and the team of Joanna Kilmartin and Steve Cox, who did first versions of *The Invincible* and *Solaris*, respectively, out of German and French rather than Polish, they too should be honored as brave astronauts sailing in the galaxy of linguistic improbability.

came from American hippies. I also liked other SF writers better than Lem did, though when I finally came across his disparaging essays it helped confirm (as did my exposure to creative writing instruction at college) that I should consider this a shameful appetite.

Better to align with the international fabulators. There was a problem, however. One of the writers in my litany was not like the others. Cortázar wasn't interested in rockets and robots, Carter ignored astronauts, and though Calvino sometimes wrote about particle physics, he made no claims for his futurological prowess. Abe wasn't, as the dust jacket of Lem's *Cyberiad* bragged, "co-founder of the Polish Astronautical Society," nor did he serve "on the advisory board of the Science Fiction Research Association of the College of Wooster, Ohio." And the others weren't members of the Science Fiction Writers of America. Lem was.**

"SFWA has just offered me a choice of memberships, honorary or regular," he wrote to Kandel in 1973. "A delicate matter, when all is said and done, since they are a club of morons." In another letter, his tone was self-pitying: "The fact that SF exists, and the fact that it 'sucks into itself' what I write, harms my career, of course." Amid a hail of confused accusations, SFWA revoked Lem's membership in 1976. In defense of the clan, Philip K. Dick shifted into high paranoiac gear. Demonstrating an unattractive

---

** Full disclosure: I too was a SFWA member, from approximately 1991 to 1996. They didn't kick me out. I let my membership lapse.

readiness to collaborate with the authorities he most feared, he denounced Lem in a letter to the FBI:

> Stanisław Lem in Krakow, Poland, himself a total Party functionary (I know this from his published writing and personal letters to me and to other people). For an Iron Curtain Party group—Lem is probably a composite committee rather than an individual, since he writes in several styles and sometimes reads foreign, to him, languages and sometimes does not—to gain monopoly positions of power from which they can control opinion through criticism and pedagogic essays is a threat to our whole field of science fiction and its free exchange of views and ideas.

Thomas Disch, one of SF's finest writers and most merciless critics (and another champion of Dick's writing who had the pleasure of being denounced to the FBI), was more able to keep his cool. His diagnosis was acute:

> The fatuity and self-serving nature of Lem's pronouncements on the field of SF are matched only by the slenderness of the reading on which they are based. . . . Most of the titles he cites are by those writers of the forties and fifties—Asimov, Van Vogt, Heinlein, Bradbury—whose appeal is essentially to a juvenile audience. Taxed with having dismissed American sf as a "hopeless case" without having read its best

authors, Lem . . . shifts the blame from himself to criticism in general, which has failed to establish a canon.

That his brusque dismissal of American SF touched a collective nerve only entrenched Lem's standing belief. This, essentially, matched Kurt Vonnegut's verdict: "Science fiction writers meet often, comfort and praise one another, exchange single-spaced letters of twenty pages and more, booze it up affectionately. . . . They are joiners. They are a lodge." In this jape, though, Vonnegut, too, had been glancing backward. By the seventies SF was diversifying wildly out of the (white man's) lodge, incorporating sex, drugs, and rock 'n' roll. The field began, fitfully, to mate itself with other countercultures and genres—including that most sacred of genres, "the literary."

Some of this even had to do with Lem. Ursula Le Guin and Theodore Sturgeon had endorsed him; it was an opening spirit of internationalism that had led to the SFWA invitation in the first place. A younger writer like Bruce Sterling, a founder of the cyberpunk movement and very much part of this next wave of possibility for the genre, could afford to view the tiff with comic detachment:

Lem was surgically excised from the bosom of American SF back in 1976. Since then plenty of other writers have quit SFWA, but those flung out for the crime of being a commie rat-bastard have remained remarkably few. . . . Recently a collection of Lem's critical essays, *Microworlds*, has appeared in paperback. For those of us not privy to the squabble these essays caused in the '70s, it makes some eye-opening reading.

> Lem compares himself to Crusoe, stating (accurately) that he
> had to erect his entire structure of "science fiction" essentially
> from scratch. He did have the ancient shipwrecked hulls of
> Wells and Stapledon at hand, but he raided them for tools
> years ago. . . . These essays are the work of a lonely man.

Sterling himself is Lem-like, capable of awesome feats of sustained extrapolation, while relatively uninterested in depicting individual human subjects. Plainly an admirer, he nevertheless can't quit poking the bear: "Lem's mind was clearly blown by reading Dick, and he struggles to find some underlying weltanschauung that would reduce Dick's ontological raving to a coherent floorplan. It's a doomed effort, full of condescension and confusion, like a ballet-master analyzing James Brown."

Sterling's basic insight is on target. Alone in Poland, with rumors of a burgeoning English-language movement reaching his ears, Lem seems to have guessed at what a serious fiction based on technological speculation would resemble, and willed himself to equal it. He extrapolated, in other words, from the examples of Wells and Stapledon. What he finally read, after delays in translation, struck him as puerile. The second half of his writing life was spent writing in anger and disappointment at the association, and to exalt himself above it.

Really, Lem should have had his mind blown not only by Philip K. Dick, but by Samuel Delany's *Stars in My Pocket like Grains of Sand*, by Le Guin's *The Dispossessed*, by Octavia Butler and Afrofuturism, by Sterling and cyberpunk, by Kim Stanley

Robinson and so many others. He lived long enough to have seen how Carter Scholz, in *Radiance*, marries a Lemian satire of Cold War militaristic capitalism to the architecture of a William Gaddis novel, or how Ted Chiang's brainy novellas crystalize Lemian themes of metacognition and first contact.

Such encounters might have challenged Lem's biases. They might also have pushed him to confront limits in his experience, exhibited in his retrograde thinking concerning women, queerness, race. But one can't force older writers to read younger ones. Robinson, in a fond and erudite introduction to a new gathering of Lem's tales, *The Truth and Other Stories*, suggests that it may have been a "willed blindness":

> Possibly he enjoyed the feeling of working alone, as many artists do, especially when they are working in a genre with an intense group dynamic that is best avoided, a genre despised by mainstream culture. Best then to find or invent your island. . . . Thus Lem's own work helped to make a change in Western culture that he himself could not see.

Lem was as skilled at the construction of his lonely island as at the construction of worlds unseen. From another of his letters to Kandel: "Lem's Three Laws proclaim: 1) nobody reads anything; 2) if they read, they don't understand anything; 3) if they read and understand, they instantly forget." This letter is dated February 1978, four months before I visited the New York Coliseum with my grandmother.

#

In *Kafka: Toward a Minor Literature*, Gilles Deleuze and Félix Guattari introduce a notion of "minority," with Kafka a preeminent example: that sense in which a writer might be positioned as not-majoritarian—that is, not a fascist, at the deepest level. Their description centers on "deterritorialization": a marginality in relation to the language or culture of the dominant. Kafka, a Czech Jew writing in German, was the very picture of deterritorialization. From this, according to Deleuze and Guattari, sprang a sensibility which ceaselessly traces power, the script running beneath the everyday.

Lem was born a Polish Jew in Lviv, a town which had just three years before his birth been part of the Austro-Hungarian state of Galicia, and so close to Ukraine that it was destined, after some border wrangling, to be Ukrainian.†† He lived, barely, through those convulsions Kafka skirted by his early death. The brutality of Nazi occupation, the Polish death camps, the succession of openly murderous fascism with the cementing of postwar Soviet bloc social and ideological controls—they all shaped Lem. He smuggles into *His Master's Voice* a portion of his own wartime experiences in Lviv's "prison pogrom" of July 1941:

> He was pulled off the street, a random pedestrian. They were
> shooting people in groups, in the yard of a prison recently

---

†† AKA, depending on language and jurisdiction, Lvov, Lwów, Lemberik and—Lemburg!

shelled and with one wing still burning. Rappaport gave me the details of the operation very calmly. The executing itself could not be seen by those herded against the building, which heated their backs like a giant oven; the shooting was done behind a broken wall. Some of those waiting, like him, for his turn, fell into a kind of stupor; others tried to save themselves—in mad ways. . . .

He remembered a young man who, rushing up to a German gendarme, howled that he was not a Jew—but howled it in Yiddish, probably because he knew no German. Rappaport felt the insane comedy of the situation, and suddenly the most precious thing to him was to preserve to the end the integrity of his mind, which would enable him to maintain an intellectual distance from the scene around him. . . . Since that was altogether impossible, he decided to believe in reincarnation. Maintaining the belief for fifteen or twenty minutes would be sufficient.

The anecdote continues for five astonishing pages, a seeming total digression from the plot, which concerns Lem's typical theme of failed communication across the cosmic gulf. Yet it concludes with the Lem stand-in Rappaport's reflection on the actions of a Nazi officer:

Although he spoke to us, you see, we were not people. He knew that we comprehended human speech but that nevertheless we were not human; he knew this quite well.

> Therefore, even if he had wanted to explain things to us, he could not have. The man could do with us what he liked, but he could not enter into negotiations, because for negotiation you must have a party at least some respects equal to the party who initiates it, and in that yard there were only he and his men. A logical contradiction, yes, but he acted according to that contradiction, and scrupulously.

Elsewhere, Lem compares this incident to Dostoyevsky's last-minute reprieve from a firing squad, which transformed his outlook forever. In the hours following his improbable survival, Lem was made to clear the corpses choking the streets. Yet his only memoir, the brief *Highcastle* (1966), says nothing of the war. It's like a tiny version of Sartre's *The Words*, focusing entirely on the inner life of a dreamy, philosophical child. It also contains not a single matzoh or latke. Lem's habit of deemphasizing all Jewish identity—a survival trait—persisted through his life. It was left to Polish Lem scholar Agnieszka Gajewska, in *The Holocaust and the Stars* (2016), to uncover the extent of the trauma Lem declined to wear on his sleeve, including the murder of much of his extended family in the Belzec camp or in the streets.

My Jewish grandmother, the Queensboro Library trustee, was just eight years older than Lem, whose weird-looking books made her so suspicious that day. She and Lem could have been cousins. Her family was from Lancut, a Polish town two hours away, another scene of Polish resistance and Jewish murder—but her parents had immigrated to the Lower East Side a few years before she was born. There they ran a candy store, just like Isaac Asimov's parents, who'd fled Russia for Brooklyn. Had Lem's parents fled, he too could have grown up in a New York candy store, eating halvah from a barrel, reading early pulp magazines. He could have been my grandfather. He could have been Asimov.

As a teenager I found the burdens of Jewish trauma unappealing yet felt them heavily nonetheless. Lem resembled other midcentury artists whose sensibilities were especially resonant to me in those years, men who ironized or allegorized midcentury cataclysms and the Cold War fear that emerged—Stanley Kubrick, Philip K. Dick, Rod Serling, J.G. Ballard. Yet unlike Kubrick, Serling, Dick, Ballard (or my grandmother), Lem was trapped on the far side of the war's result, submitting his drafts to Soviet censor boards, seeing the results promoted for the Nobel Prize by KGB agents, left only to be able to guess at which rumors of capitalist corruption or enviable Western freedoms might be hype, and which might contain some truth.

Lem's satires of capitalism, fused to his prescience, are so acute that they glimpse the present horizon. In *Bullshit Jobs* (2019), the anthropologist and anarchist organizer David Graeber retells a Lem parable:

> Space voyager Ijon Tichy describes a visit to a planet inhabited by a species to which the author gives the rather unsubtle name of Phools. At the time of his arrival the Phools were experiencing a classic Marxian overproduction crisis. . . . "Through the ages inventors built machines

that simplified work, and where in ancient times a hundred Drudgelings had bent their sweating backs, centuries later a few stood by a machine. Our scientists improved the machines, and the people rejoiced at this, but subsequent events show how cruelly premature was that rejoicing." . . . The factories, ultimately, became a little too efficient, and one day an engineer created machines that could operate with no supervision at all. . . . Before long, the Drudgelings, though—as Tichy's interlocutor insisted, entirely free to do what they wanted provided they did not interfere in anyone else's property rights—were dropping like flies. Much heated debate ensued, and a succession of failed half measures. The Phools' high council, the Plenum Moronicum, attempted to replace the Drudgelings as consumers as well, by creating robots that would eat, use, and enjoy all the products the New Machines produced far more intensely than any living being could possibly do, while also materializing money to pay for it. But this was unsatisfying. Finally, realizing a system where both production and consumption were being done by machines was rather pointless, they concluded the best solution would be for the entire population to render itself—entirely voluntarily—to the factories to be converted into beautiful shiny disks and arranged in pleasant patterns across the landscape.

Not that increased exposure to the West's failings softened Lem's view of Stalinism's legacy. From a letter to Kandel:

Say one country permits eating little children, right before the eyes of crazed mothers, and another permits eating absolutely anything, whereupon it turns out that the majority of people in that country eat shit. So what, does the fact that most people eat shit demonstrate . . . that it is *better* to eat children alive?

Lem's most Dr. Strangelovian or Alphavillian book, *Memoirs Found in a Bathtub*, was easily my favorite for years. The entire book is narrated from within a gigantic structure known only as "the Building," a hive of espionage, paranoia, and corruption clearly meant to stand as some unholy amalgam of the Pentagon and Lubyanka, the headquarters of the KGB. The narrator reels from department to department, attempting to grasp the Building's workings and his place within it, as though Kafka's *Castle* has been turned inside out: now, instead of a place impossible to enter, it is akin to the Hotel California, or life on earth. Death is the only exit.

Rather than dividing the human universe between Castle and Village, as in Kafka, all that seems to exist outside the Building is another structure. This, its evil counterpart, the Anti-Building, remains unseen and lurking. In this reduced universe, the actions of eavesdropping, decryption, and interrogation have engulfed the human realm entirely. Every character must at some point be scrutinized, or self-scrutinize, for the risk of being a concealed agent of the Anti-Building. Have the populations merged and mingled for years? A kind of singsong work chant erupts from time to time to explain the fundament of this universe:

*What makes the Building go?*
*The Anti-Building makes it go!*

The book's symbolic architecture makes it a perfect rebus of Lem's baseline theme of the problem of an encounter with an Other, that which he rehearses in his stories of disastrous first contact with aliens. The dream and nightmare of our connection to some unfathomable variation on ourselves dooms us to solipsism. In *Memoirs*, Lem's spies are entrenched in a paranoid equivalent of the anthropomorphism that circumscribes the search for extraterrestrial intelligence: the only index available for the possible activities of the Anti-Building is within themselves. Yet by looking there, they locate only the madness of their own search for self-definition. There may be an echo here of Italian philosopher Giorgio Agamben's thesis in *The Open*: human political states depend on the identification of a dehumanized other against which to define themselves. Agamben locates the origin of this process in the fundamental definition of "the human" as "not the animal." Yet, as everyone knows, the human *is* the animal, and as Pogo tells us in Walt Kelly's comic strip, "We have met the enemy and he is us."

This year, I felt, sadly, that *Memoirs Found in a Bathtub* was better to recall and recap than actually reread. I found myself impatient with the frenetic satirical set-pieces that make up the narrator's journey. Lem as a humorist can be giddily surreal, but just as often works with blunt instruments ("Phools"). His serial targets in *Memoirs*—organized Christianity, self-referential academic scholarship, the state security apparatus—are fish in a barrel, ones which Lem, rather than shooting, hammers to death. At the same time, Lem shies from other interrogations: men and women, parents and children, the nuclear family, those psycho-sexual excavations that galvanize Kafka's power to disquiet us at the deepest levels. Lem doesn't move beyond the place that has mistakenly defined Kafka in the popular imagination: a dissection of the twentieth-century paranoid bureaucratic state. It is natural then that Graeber, bureaucracy's jubilant enemy, was a fan.

If Lem Two—the allegorist and satirist—was a bit of a let-down to me this year, however, Lem One, the hard SF writer, only soared.

#

The three midperiod masterworks *Solaris*, *The Invincible*, and *His Master's Voice*, and Lem's final novel, *Fiasco*, exhibit an uncanny density of purpose. They sound a bit like H.P. Lovecraft, in a story like "The Colour Out of Space," where men's minds (and it is, always, men) are shown to be incapable of grappling with the Something Out There, their certainties shattered, their mental, moral, and emotional tools bent back on themselves by the implications of the unknowable knowledge exploding in their heads. Unlike Lovecraft, Lem didn't offer up a sexy beast like the octopoid menace Cthulhu. His dispassionate treatment of the theme may have circumscribed his popular audience (as Jarett Kobek quipped, "You don't see a lot of *Solaris* bumper stickers out there"), but the lonely achievement of these books is exactly what

Lem claimed: a science fiction both philosophical and literary, and worthy, at last, of its name.

*The Invincible* is the simplest of these books. The encounter the explorers of this book must suffer is with a world of swarming microscopic robots. These, likely a misguided attempt at a military defense technology which have outlived their makers, have gained a kind of "life," if not consciousness, sheerly by the encompassing persistence with which they occupy their homeworld and repel the inquiry of visitors. They present both a dwarfing existential rebuke to human pretentions and a grim logistical challenge to the fallible instrument of the human body. Lem's genius is to make the outward adventure, detailed in breathtaking set-pieces and on dazzling scale, a perfect emblem of the philosophical theme. The spoiler is the title.

In *Reverse Colonization: Science Fiction, Imperial Fantasy, and Alt-victimhood* (2021), David Higgins shows how consistently American and British SF engages in reverse-engineering of colonial themes, bargaining against imperial guilt to dabble in possibilities for exoneration. In this damning thesis, SF is more than a little culpable for the way all actors in the political arena confidently define themselves as in rebellion against some evil empire—everyone a Millennium Falcon shrieking against the Death Star. Lem's use of the typical iconography of explorers and settlers is more glum, his SF born outside US techno-triumphalism. Nor is it tinged like the rueful fading empires of British SF, the crushed nobility of John Wyndham, Michael Moorcock, and J.G. Ballard. His astronauts and technicians aren't innocent of all imperial guilt, but it smolders within a damp core of endured compromise and guilt, the dourness of Polish national character. They're workers at tasks, grateful for the most incremental of solutions, and relieved at the distance the stars provide from insoluble perplexities and sorrows back on earth (or, presumably, from a job in a Soviet-era factory or bureaucracy). Lem's astronauts are depressed.

Where are the women? As with hardboiled detectives, women in Lem may be lodged bitterly in an astronaut's past; yet it is essentially only in *Solaris* that they erupt into the tale at hand. Lem said the book presented itself to him unconsciously, suggesting a kind of return of the repressed (at times, he muttered awkward covering statements about their absence from his books by saying that women simply didn't belong in space). *Solaris,* his purest study of human limitation, is therefore also his most self-implicating.

The ocean planet that gives *Solaris* its title is, like the mechanized planet of *The Invincible*, a total symbol of the incomprehensible Other. When the protagonist Kelvin arrives at a space station hovering above it, the planet's alien brain presents him with a gift or puzzle or test: an almost-perfect simulacrum of his lover, who committed suicide after they'd quarreled. The simulacrum loves him implacably, knowing nothing of its origin or past. This convergence of symbols in Ocean-Planet-Other-Woman would seem almost disastrously overheated, but (even in the famously problematic translation) one can see Lem stripping his style back to an existentialist restraint as lucid as Camus's.

In the lore of American SF, Tom Godwin's short story "The Cold Equations" (1954) has been enshrined as a kind of quintessence of the genre. In it, a space pilot discovers a stowaway, a young girl, on a vessel ferrying medicine to a needful planet. The problem is that her weight overbalances the ship. They'll never reach their destination alive. Cold equations dictate the foolish girl's ejection from the airlock; after some handwringing, and a farewell call to her brother, the dirty, unavoidable task is done. The brutal, silly exercise was seen as an example of the hard truths SF ought to encode.

Whether Lem knew Godwin's story or not, he swallows the tale, with its bitter pill of hostility, into *Solaris*. The simulacrum wife provided by the alien world-entity both entrances and horrifies Kelvin, and he impulsively shoves her out of the station into space. This solves nothing: the planet simply prints another copy for Kelvin to live with, if he can. His lover is now a suicide, a murder victim, and alive, or undead, as well as an intimate sample of the alien material to which he has devoted years of study. Kelvin, despite himself, allows himself to begin to return her love; she reaches into him, even if she has been made only out of parts of his own mind.

What Updike called Lem's "sheer love of compilation" expresses itself in a rapturous cataloguing of the manifold upwellings, outcroppings and metastases of the planet's brain-like surface. And in a chapter called "Solaristics," Lem indexes the contents of the station's library, which consists of neglected tomes of scientific speculation on the planet's origin and purposes. Each Solarist disproves the last; all will be humbled by the final enigma of their chosen topic of study. The catalogue of discredited Solarists forecasts the fictional reviews and introductions Lem will begin writing ten years later.

As Solaris the planet lures Solarists, so the suggestive conundrum of *Solaris* the novel beckons scholars, moths to its flame. "The strong suggestion of this novel . . . that earthly academic categories are rendered ludicrous by the living ocean," writes Brooks Landon in *Science Fiction after 1900*. Istvan Csicsery-Ronay Jr., in *The Seven Beauties of Science Fiction*, adds, as if from the same chorus, "Solaris . . . dislodges anthropocentrism without providing any means to recoup the loss. By not responding, by being arelational, the planet illuminates humanity's need to be in relation to some other intelligence. . . . It removes hope from the novum, leaving only the reinforcement of the negative historical processes of humanity." Carl Freedman, in *Critical Theory and Science Fiction*, concludes:

> The extreme otherness of the ocean cannot be directly shown but must function as the relatively blank center of the novel whose nature the reader tries, with considerable difficulty, to infer from what the other *does*. Accordingly, literary criticism of Lem's novel is a particularly fascinating yet also frustrating activity; the text itself is unusually insistent upon the provisionality and partiality of every reading and especially upon every construction of the ocean itself.

These elegant labors under the light of Lem's impossible object almost seem enclosed within the novel itself, further volumes for the space station's library. Kim Stanley Robinson puts it most simply: "His masterpiece *Solaris* . . . renders unnecessary any more alien stories. Nothing further can be said on this topic . . . Possibly it can be said that when one feels the urge for such a thing one should simply reread *Solaris* and learn its lessons again."

What then was left for Lem to add in *His Master's Voice,* and in his last novel, *Fiasco*, both tales of scientific quests to meet and interpret the alien Other? As the Solarist Snow announces, "We have no needs of other worlds. We need mirrors. . . . A single world, our own, suffices, but we can't accept it for what it is." *His Master's Voice* and *Fiasco* are those mirrors. Quests for the alien become occasions for Lem's study of the limits of human inquiry, and of the problem that had come increasingly to obsess him, of human evil. The Hannah Arendt in Lem had seeped to the surface; satiric demolitions of knavery were no longer sufficient. These later books make a determined study of the corruption of reason by avarice, of science by paranoid militarism. The human species' collective fervor for an encounter with the unknown reveals itself as a cover on nihilism, our urge to destroy.

*Fiasco* is the angrier book and the more unruly. A final statement on his great theme, it's clotted with digressive meta-stories, recursive arguments, and breathtaking set-pieces, as if Lem wanted to feel and exhibit, one last time, all of which he was capable. Pirx the Pilot dies, either at the end of the first chapter or in the last lines of the book—the puzzle is a deliberate provocation to anyone interested in Lem's sense of identification with his longest-lived character. How could such things matter in the face of the news about sentience that Lem has been placed on earth to deliver?

*His Master's Voice* (1967) may, however, be the more perfect enunciation. It concerns, simply, a long epitaph for the failed project of analyzing a single enigmatic radio message from another galaxy. The book's demoralized researchers are engaged in a version of Solaristics while bereft of a Solaris, like a *Moby-Dick* written by a crew who will never know what a whale looks like, yet are, somehow, still destined to be destroyed by one. In the background of the science stands the politics: militarists eager to understand whether the message can be translated into a Doomsday Device. The book is essayistic and ruminative and may seem at first like a slab of sheer cognition, yet it delivers, paradoxically, a deeper self-portrait than that glimpsed in Lem's brief gnomic memoir, or in his discursive autobiographical essays. The novel's vain yet self-flaying scientist-narrator builds to heights of scorn, sorrow, and self-reproach verging on those of Robert Musil's protagonist Ulrich in *The Man without Qualities*.

From Michael Kandel's translation:

> I was never able to conquer the distance between persons. An animal is fixed to its here-and-now by the senses, but man manages to detach himself, to remember, to sympathize with others, to visualize their states of mind and feelings: this, fortunately, is not true. In such attempts at pseudo merging and transferal we are only able, imperfectly, darkly, to visualize ourselves. What would happen to us if we

could truly sympathize with others, feel with them, suffer for them? The fact that human anguish, fear, and suffering melt away with the death of the individual, that nothing remains of the ascents, the declines, the orgasms, and the agonies, is a praiseworthy gift of evolution, which made us like the animals. If from every unfortunate, from every victim, there remained even a single atom of his feelings, if thus grew the inheritance of the generations, if even a spark could pass from man to man, the world would be full of raw, bowel-torn howling.

Happy birthday.

# Calvino's "Lightness" and the Feral Child of History

I SPEAK AS A feral child of Gowanus. That is to say not the synonym for a currently fashionable bar or restaurant but a broken city, in a broken time. I couldn't have been granted a sufficient precognition to believe how my appetite for connection through cultural things—through songs, stories, films, and paintings—would lead me into such a stately position as that in which I appear before you. I figured I'd be destined to stay feral—that it was in fact my appetites that would keep me so. But look at me now: like the stray cat in Paula Fox's *Desperate Characters*, set and written a few blocks from where I grew up, I've been lured indoors, into some kind of respectable position, into a condition of patronage. The risk is to be rendered harmless, of course.

Whether harmless or not, inside I remain a creature of those streets. I piece together fragments to make my armor (now I'm a knight, not a cat, but a knight like Tweedledee or Tweedledum). I don't want to conceal that I'm piecing together this present confession (a kind of manifesto-just-for-today, it seems to me) from such stuff. It's made primarily from portions of two talks I wrote and delivered, shortly after the election of November 2016. That autumn was, for my writing, otherwise a kind of Death Valley, until the time in mid-January when I began to be able to assemble a fiction again, a novel called *The Feral Detective*. In those weeks I was asked, fortuitously, to comment on Italo Calvino's essay "Lightness," and so I began to read him again. Also fortuitously, if banally, I was asked to comment in several forums on the artist's position in the atrocious new age that was dawning (or which had had its face revealed, as in the original meaning of William S. Burroughs's title *Naked Lunch*: "That frozen moment when everyone sees what is on the ends of their forks"). These fragments won't fit. The more I try to make them say, the more I uncover their insufficiency. I'm destined to abandon rather than finish this project, but why should I wait until my death to publish an unfinished work?

A joke: One day a tiny man entered a café and said, "I want a double caramel mocha latte, very hot and very sweet," adding: "I'm not going to pay, because I'm not afraid of anyone." He drank his coffee and didn't pay. The café owner said nothing, as he was afraid of scandal. But when the tiny man repeated the trick a few times, the café owner said: "I've had it. I'll get a tough guy to beat up the tiny man if he comes back." So, on the fourth day, when the tiny man said, "I want a double caramel mocha latte, very hot, very sweet," the tough guy goes to him and says: "So you're afraid of no one?" "That's right." "Well, neither am I." "Well," says the tiny man, "make that two double caramel mocha lattes, very hot and very sweet!"

That joke operates in a way that, for me, the best jokes do—by delivering the listener, at the moment of experiencing the punch line, from a state of tension, into a kind of existential abyss of possibilities. The little man's surprising reaction opens a trapdoor for an escape from the obvious. What will happen? Will they in fact become friends? What would it mean if everyone were to discover within themselves an absolute lack of fear in the face of what seems an unavoidable conflict? Could there possibly be enough double caramel mocha latte to go around?

The joke's source is Jean-Luc Godard's *Alphaville*, a film from 1965, made a year after I was born. I first saw it in a repertory movie house in New York City when I was sixteen, and it immediately became a cherished object for me. Much like my consideration of Calvino to come, the joke raises the problem of translation; I encountered it in French with English subtitles. I don't speak, or read, French or Italian. And I've taken liberties with the language in making the joke my own. This is what novelists do, take liberties, make things their own. *Alphaville*, in truth, supplied me with more than a joke. It might be said that it supplied me with my first novel, *Gun, with Occasional Music*, since the film portrays a hard-boiled detective who investigates a crime in a dystopian city of the future.

In Godard's variation on my novel, the government seems to have ceded power to a gigantic financial computer, a computer operated by impassive scientists who've grown completely indifferent to human emotions such as love and sorrow. It's a romantic film. The detective falls in love with the lead scientist's beautiful daughter, in an archetypal plot that evokes Shakespeare's *Tempest* (and therefore also the American SF film *Forbidden Planet*, though

Godard may have been oblivious to this). It's also a very funny film, despite its terrifying vision. Like George Orwell's *Nineteen Eighty-Four*, or an episode of Rod Serling's *The Twilight Zone*, or the Wachowskis' film *The Matrix*, or nearly any other effective dystopian narrative, *Alphaville* derives its power and relevance not so much from a prediction of a distant future as from a metaphoric distillation of a condition of the present—the present experienced by the artist, the writer or filmmaker, and understood, at least intuitively, by the reader or audience member on that level. Experienced as their world, the one they live in, given its complete name for the first time. Godard did not shoot *Alphaville* on soundstages with futuristic sets, or by using CGI; he simply placed his characters in the newest office buildings and scientific laboratories in Paris. In the simplest possible sense, Alphaville *was* Paris, in 1965—seen with new eyes. For many reasons, the most powerful insights about the present are often communicated by this defamiliarization—by setting them in a fantastic or allegorical or absurdist world, one which exaggerates some elusive quality of our experience into visibility.

This is not so different from the way a joke, or a piece of surrealism or absurdity, can lead us to the brink of the existential abyss, to an opening or rupture that is also a place where anything might be possible. Perhaps it is also not so different from the way that a three-minute pop song can break our hearts by seeming to encapsulate, in a few corny lines and gestures, a few well-worn chord progressions, the emotions that strain within us but rarely find a doorway to emerge into our everyday lives.

How does the lighter-than-air gesture of the artist, singer, filmmaker, or even the teller of a joke retain its relevance and power in times of darkness? If the artist is a citizen, obligated, in times of oppression, to acts of mutual aid, reparative justice, and participatory democracy, perhaps even of civil disobedience and personal sacrifice, what is the place of the impulse to fantasy, the playful, mercurial, polymorphous desire of the artist to generate nonutilitarian gestures of irreverence, playfulness, distraction, and delight? Perhaps it is only a residual activity, at best described as a freedom worth preserving, the evidence of whose persistence reassures us that our wish to include areas of "free play" proves the benevolence of our caretaking of the world, much as we may view the ever-diminishing presence of the art teacher in a public school—ever-diminishing yet not quite wiped out completely—as evidence of a tiny indulgence that redeems the merciless pragmatism of our Core Curriculum, our teaching-to-the-test. In this model, the artist is barely more than a child himself. Or can it possibly be that the seeming weightlessness of the artist's existence in our civil society masks a more essential, more integral purpose—one of crucial value precisely in times of precarity, political incoherence, and disillusion?

Calvino's *Six Memos for the Next Millennium*, where "Lightness" appears, was written on the occasion of an invitation to give the Charles Eliot Norton Poetry Lectures at Harvard—a sequence, always, of six talks. Only five of the six were written, when Calvino, amid preparations for his travel to America, died of a stroke, age sixty-one. Because of the subsequent publication of the memos, the nonoccurrence of his visit to Harvard has been enshrined; it forms a kind of unfinished falling to earth like that of Icarus in Brueghel's famous painting. The memos sail on forever, borne on the lightness and swiftness of Calvino's genius, but their circumstance recalls their point of origin in Calvino's living body, that heavy fact of the author's mortal person now here among us, then vanishing forever. It happens that as a part of Calvino's American voyage to deliver the lectures he had also agreed to a circumscribed "book tour" that would bring him as far as California. There, he was scheduled to read at Cody's Books, on Telegraph Avenue in Berkeley. I was then living in Berkeley, as the kind of feral creature known as an "aspiring writer," having dropped out of college and inaugurated a decade of working as a bookstore clerk. I turned up the night of Calvino's scheduled reading and learned of his death from a note pinned to the door of Cody's. This was before the instantaneity and collectivity of internet mourning. Calvino may have been dead for weeks, but he was alive in my mind, and I had been about to declare myself to him as his fan and acolyte until I walked up and read the note. Instead I turned from the bookshop door and mourned alone.

The book became Calvino's first posthumous publication; lacking the sixth memo, it also became an example of that genre to which every author fears contributing—the unfinished book. Calvino, being the most elegant of authors, left the most elegant example of an unfinished book imaginable, one which barely seems to suffer a formal disruption. Calvino's art was one of both concision and endlessness, infinitude. Like a univalve seashell-constructor, he worked by accretion, and was more prone to beginnings than endings. His writings, long or short, seem to open out, like the roofless dwellings seashells are, to a sky of pure possibility. In fact, he wrote a novel, *If on a Winter's Night a Traveler*, that consists only of first chapters of potential novels. The five memos seem complete in themselves, and yet are open-ended—and Calvino's wife Esther informs the reader in her brief introduction that Calvino had already conceived a seventh and an eighth memo, overflowing the container of the Harvard lecture format.

The grace of "Lightness," I should add, has only been amplified by the poet Geoffrey Brock's recent retranslation, the one I'll use, and which I'll try not to damage with my elisions or slight paraphrases. The memo begins with a general announcement of purposes, and then turns toward the material that so compels me:

> When I began my career, the duty of every young writer, the categorical imperative, was to represent our times. . . . I soon realized that the gap between the realities of life that were supposed to be my raw materials and the sharp, darting nimbleness that I wanted to animate my writing was becoming harder and harder for me to bridge. . . . I sometimes felt that the whole world was turning to stone: a slow petrifaction, more advanced in some people and places than in others, but from which no aspect of life was spared. It was as if no one could escape Medusa's inexorable gaze.

The only hero capable of cutting off Medusa's head is Perseus, who flies on winged sandals, Perseus, who looks not upon the Gorgon's face but only upon her image reflected in his bronze shield. . . . In order to cut off Medusa's head without being turned to stone, Perseus supports himself on the lightest of stuff—wind and clouds—and turns his gaze toward that which can be revealed to him only indirectly, by an image caught in a mirror. . . . The relationship between Perseus and the Gorgon is complex, and it doesn't end with the beheading of the monster. . . . As for the severed head, rather than abandoning it, Perseus takes it with him, hidden in a sack. When in danger of defeat, he has only to show it to his enemies. . . . Perseus masters that terrible face by keeping it hidden, just as he had earlier defeated it by looking at its reflection. In each case his power derives from refusing to look directly while not denying the reality of the world of monsters in which he must live, a reality he carries with him and bears as his personal burden.

In the weeks and months following the election I did more than take solace from these pages: I read them aloud in several settings, attempting to provide the same solace I took. I read those words to artists and writers, but also to students and scholars—all of those who, like myself, were at risk of suffering doubts as to the relevancy, the effectiveness, or the sustainability of our activities during times of great historical damage and continuing, or increasing, precariousness. Times that may have, in fact, already been very much with us, but which have lately shed their disguises, and faced us directly, daring us to let our hopes be frozen into stone.

Calvino wrote in a timeless voice precisely to invite this universal applicability, but it's worth keeping in mind the particular historical world of monsters within which Calvino, as a European, a citizen of Italy born in 1923, came of age as a writer and moralist, and as a person. The simple facts: Italo Calvino, after being conscripted into the Italian army, participated against his wishes in the World War II occupation of the French Riviera. In the words of Marjorie Perloff: "Perhaps the irony and distance of his early pieces grew out of his compulsory service with an army he opposed." In 1944, with his brother, Calvino joined the Garibaldi Brigades resistance group, joining combat against the German Army in the Alps; his parents were placed in house arrest by the Nazis in retaliation for his activities. In his account, "Political Autobiography of a Young Man," Calvino describes his mother "behaving with dignity and firmness before the SS and the Fascist militia, and in her long detention as a hostage, not least when the blackshirts three times pretended to shoot my father in front of her eyes." He added: "The historical events which mothers take part in acquire the greatness and invincibility of natural phenomena."

The Gorgon's nightmare face may include historical traumas even fresher than the midcentury fascisms that Calvino, in "Lightness" contemplated from the relative distance of 1985. The memo encourages this impression, when Calvino turns his next attention to Milan Kundera's *The Unbearable Lightness of Being*. Calvino praises Kundera for accomplishing the rare magic of "convey[ing the novelist's] idea of lightness with examples drawn from the events of contemporary life without making it the unattainable object of an endless quest." Kundera was, of course, living under the shadow of the failure of the Prague Spring, and of the Red Army's continuing occupation of Czechoslovakia, with its resultant censorship and other restrictions on basic human rights. As Calvino says: "His novel shows us how everything in life that we choose and value for its lightness quickly reveals its own unbearable heaviness. Perhaps nothing escapes this fate but the liveliness and nimbleness of the mind—the very qualities with which the novel is written, qualities that belong to a universe other than the one we live in."

Calvino further characterizes Kundera's book as "a bitter declaration of the Ineluctable Weight of Living—living not only with the desperate and all-pervading state of oppression that was the fate of his unlucky country, but with the human condition shared also by us, however much luckier we may be." It's here in this remark that the clue hides, the inkling I want to explore. We shouldn't let this clue slip past us despite its elusiveness—Calvino hides it in his evocation of the world's outer darkness, the monstrousness of politics and history, of collective oppressions. It's the blandly universal phrase "the human condition."

In that discretion, we've encountered Calvino's typical reticence about confessional writing. Autobiography was the literary mode Calvino trusted least to deliver the goods, once famously remarking: "Once you start down the road to autobiography, where do you stop?" Indeed, in "Lightness," embedded in the long passage I read, lies another clue: "Perseus comes to my aid even now, as I begin to feel caught in a grip of stone, as happens whenever I try to mix the historical and the autobiographical." Here, it seems to me, the Gorgon threatening to overtake "Lightness" lies not only on the perimeter or horizon, in the realm of the historical or political, but within. The monster's face stares at Calvino from the inside.

Elsewhere in the second of the memos, entitled "Quickness," Calvino reflects that he is—in what has become a famous quote—"a Saturn who dreamed he was a Mercury." Yet in Brock's new translation, these words are rendered as "I am a Saturnine man who wants to be mercurial." The retranslation lures the implication—that of a depressive or morbid temperament—further out of the shadows. The Saturnine man is ringed in his own gloom; Saturn is a planet possessing its own unbearable weight. The Saturnine man may have some difficulty getting out of bed in the morning. Any reader of Calvino will recognize the depths of underlying remorse evoked, paradoxically, by his gifts of lightness.

I apologize to Calvino for my probing in this area, which I need to continue doing. In an essay called "By Way of an Autobiography," which lasts for a scant three pages, he writes: "Having grown up in times of dictatorship, and being overtaken by total war when of military age, I still have the notion that to live in peace and freedom is a frail kind of good fortune that might be taken from me in an instant."

In his interview for the *Paris Review* (an interview that was, like the memos, both interrupted and incomplete, perhaps a further reflection of Calvino's ambivalence about both completion and confession), he describes his life after the war:

> My whole life really began after the war. Before that I lived in San Remo, which is far removed from literary and cultural circles. When deciding to move, I hesitated between Turin and Milan. . . . For a long time I couldn't choose between the two cities. Perhaps if I had chosen Milan, which is a more active, livelier city, things would have been different. Turin is a more serious, more austere place. The choice of Turin was, to some extent, an ethical one—I identified with its cultural and political tradition. Turin had been the city of the anti-Fascist intellectuals, and this appealed to that part of me fascinated by a kind of Protestant severity. It is the most Protestant city of Italy, an Italian Boston. Perhaps because of my surname [Calvino is Italian for Calvin], and perhaps because I come from a very austere family, I was predestined to make moralistic choices. When I was six, in San Remo, my very first elementary school was a private Protestant institution. The teachers stuffed me full of scripture. So I have a certain internal conflict: I feel a kind of opposition toward the more carefree, slipshod Italy, which has made me identify with those Italian thinkers who believe that the country's misfortunes come from having missed the Protestant Reformation. On the other hand, my disposition is not at all that of a puritan. My surname is Calvino but my given name, after all, is Italo.

One last piece of evidence, one last theft from the private Calvino, comes in a short story he himself acknowledged was a rare instance of direct autobiography, called "Into the War." Here, the young Calvino steals a glimpse of Mussolini himself, driving by in a motorcade: "The war was here, the war he had declared, and he was in a car with his generals; he had a new uniform. . . . And as though it were some sort of a game, he sought only the complicity of other people—not too much to ask—so much so that people were tempted to allow him it, in order not to spoil his party: in fact one almost felt a sting of remorse at knowing that we were more adult than he was, in not wanting to play his game."

Here the soberly Protestant Calvino, an old soul in a young man's body, understands natively that the dictator who has thrust his country into disaster is cursed or blessed with a kind of *savage* lightness—an infantile incapacity for introspection or remorse, a gleeful ignorance of the depths of the abyss on which the human realm is perched, an abyss into which the leader has never gazed, nor allowed to gaze into him.

This raises the specter of our current Gorgon, but I'll leave him unnamed, for a little while yet.

Instead, let me turn to my own confession. Unlike Calvino, after a period of avoiding being direct and confessional in my novels and stories, I've turned out not to be shy about autobiography in fiction, though I can confirm his anxieties—once you start, how do you stop? In fact, once I started, I realized I'd never had any choice in the matter, and that the earlier work I believed was devised to avoid autobiography was as transparent as the later work which embraced it—especially if one read the earlier work in light of the confessions that followed. I'm shy about comparing myself to one of the twentieth century's greatest writers. But the least I can do, having invaded Calvino's privacy, is invade my own.

I was born in 1964. I came of age in a country at war and under the shadow of a paranoiac administration, one famous for an enemies list which, if it had been thorough, would certainly have included not only my parents but practically every adult I'd ever met. My parents and their friends straggled into the 1970s attempting to articulate and extend the accomplishments of a utopian cultural participation already tattered around the edges before the phenomenal blowback of the gaudy, reactionary Reagan era. That propositional utopian zone was, for me, as precious as it was incoherent, as seductive as it was incomplete, as virtuous as it was unsustainable as a place to live—not least because for me it was being enacted, in the form of a handful of experimental communes in brownstones in the newly named Boerum Hill, within the wider catastrophe zone of Abe Beame's New York, a nationally abandoned city where whole precincts were on fire and intrepid artists and children picked gaily through the lawless rubble, rescuing or creating objects of dire fascination.

Perseus might have gazed at my childhood only in the reflection in his shield, but I kind of liked it.

And my first appetite for art was for articulations of the dark, for Gorgon faces I could meet with my own level gaze. Europeans like Franz Kafka, Max Ernst, Fritz Lang, George Orwell, Anna Kavan, Stanisław Lem, who translated European fascism into symbolism or allegory seemed to stir a particular recognition in me, as well as American Cold War art like film noir, Stanley Kubrick, Rod Serling's *Twilight Zone*, and Jack Kirby's comic books—so much of this art created by men who'd served as soldiers in World War II—or the morbid science fiction of Philip K. Dick and J.G. Ballard, or an album like Talking Heads' *Fear of Music*. The list goes on—I've worn it on my sleeve, no need to recite it again now.

When it came time for me to fashion my own description of the world, I reached, instinctively, for dystopia and postapocalypse. Not one or the other, but, as in my novels *Amnesia Moon* and *Chronic City*, both at the same time, even at the risk of an incoherence of my own. For me, dystopia and postapocalypse were like ebony and ivory, or peanut butter and chocolate, two great tastes that go great together, or rather, two modes which only *in conjunction* form the sufficient preconditions for a description of the world as I saw it. A collapsing world, that was, where, under the shadow of history, temporary arrangements of family or friends, or perhaps a family made of friends, cleared a little space and—well, what they did, as often as not, was make a spaghetti dinner, or light a joint, or put on the soundtrack LP to *The Harder They Come* and roll up the carpet and dance. Or possibly all three.

Believe it or not, this peculiar tableau—dystopia, and postapocalypse, and dancing under the shadow of both— forms the *easy* description, and the easier part of my own coming-of-age to face. In the middle of my childhood, when I was eleven, my mother became sick with a brain tumor, suffered a series of seizures and two brain operations. She died when I was fourteen. This loss was catastrophic, an iceberg-wrecking as if suffered by a *Titanic* which never completely sinks but is always and forever sinking. Yet one of the mysteries in this loss is the degree to which in my grasp of it then (or, I concede, perhaps in my retroactive falsification of my grasp of it then) it was also *obvious*. I received my mother's death as a dark memo, a confirmation of a suspicion I already held about existence. *Of course* something unfathomable, a blot on the universe, was coming to swallow up what you loved most and what loved you most. This happening was always foretold, was always a given. *Of course* the arrangements of home and family were always tenuous, etched in gossamer, tinted in nostalgia even while they occurred, like my parents' worn gatefold copy of *Sgt. Pepper*, which was missing its cardboard cut-out Beatle dolls. That band you're grooving to? The one that models the perfect gestalt of endearing human types, working in selfless harmony? They already broke up, man.

Here's where, surprisingly, I find myself experiencing a deep resonance with Calvino's self-portraiture. Why should the feral child of Gowanus, the paisley-diaper baby of hippie parents, identify with the sober Calvinistic moralist Calvino describes—the young man who chose Turin over Milan, the Saturnine personality who must grapple toward the mercurial, who must make an *active* pursuit of lightness?

It is in this obscure zone of inquiry that I locate the part of me which took my mother's death as kind of cosmic justice, a deep affirmation of my own mordant apprehensions about the human condition. In fact, despite certain appearances, like, say, a fringe vest and batik T-shirt, I was a furtive, serious, judgmental child. As a teenager, I resembled a kind of literary Goth—I remember my father's surprise when he found me dragging around a volume of Schopenhauer. Was it merely because I'd internalized the condition of collapse all around me—the dystopian city, the crooked regime in disgrace, the retreat of the Age of Aquarius ideals from their transformative vanguard? Was it a trace inheritance from my father's midwestern Protestantism? Was it instilled in me in my participation in Quaker Sunday School, and my years among the silent reverent Society of Friends?

Here, I begin to fumble at introspection's atrium, hesitating at those twin doors marked "nature" and "nurture." My darkness feels native to me, inborn, something waited to be activated and uncovered by my experience and my reading, both. But perhaps there's another influence. My grandmother, a woman who walked the earth as a kind of collapsed star of disappointment, who by the time I knew her had suffered at least three violent divorces: from the Jewish God of her family inheritance, and in whom she found it impossible to believe even if it divided her from her family and culture; from the secular God of Marxist belief, which if it survived in her had been reduced and silenced by the serial humiliations of the twentieth century's betrayals of its ideals; and from my grandfather, who stole her youth.

Yes, it might be her, standing there at the crossroads of nature and nurture. My grandmother instilled in me a truly catastrophic definition of the Jewish identity I'd unwillingly inherited. It worked this way: first, I couldn't possibly *be* Jewish, not in any way that sustained or enlightened, me, not in a way that attached me to any community of meaning or belief, because I came from a twin-layered legacy of disbelievers, herself and my own mother; because I'd never entered a synagogue or made myself remotely eligible for bar mitzvah; because my father had pulled me into Quakerism—but second, that at the exact same time I was absolutely Jewish in the sole imperishable sense that when the Nazis came, they'd pin the yellow star on me and drag me away. In that one sense, I belonged, I was marked. And, she made me certain, I shouldn't fail to be vigilant: the Nazis *were* coming.

No wonder I was ready to discover Kafka, guilty as I was of a crime I not only hadn't committed but was incapable of committing.

A marvelous and disturbing development in clinical psychology, in the study of attachment and human development, is the revelation that profound trauma may skip a generation, to impart itself not in the child but in the grandchild. It's unsurprising that the study which popularized this notion was entitled "The Intergenerational Transmission of Increased Anxiety Traits in Third-Generation Holocaust Survivors." Not that my grandmother had been a direct survivor of the camps, but believe me, she took the Holocaust personally; she was a vehicle of grievance capacious enough to carry an entire century's worth. She was at least a train. Whether this theory is ultimately destined to be exposed as folklore or not, it seems to point me to the fact of some identification across time, past the Aquarian generation, to some midcentury version of self that is more existentially reserved, disturbed, and hesitant. This kinship across generations that I experienced in knowing my grandmother, and in recognizing her severity within myself, I explored in a novel called *Dissident Gardens*. Strangely, then, Calvino's war, and Fritz Lang's and Jack Kirby's and Rod Serling's war, may still be my own, may be the only war. His formative trauma, my formative trauma. I don't mean to suggest I've ever been in uniform, any more than my grandmother was interned at a concentration camp—let alone that I served on both sides of World War II, a fact which, it occurs to me now, makes Calvino somewhat like a character in a dark historical picaresque, like Jack Crabb, in Thomas Berger's *Little Big Man*, who manages to operate both as a member of Custer's cavalry and of Sitting Bull's raiders during the Battle of Little Big Horn.

The lasting relevance of Calvino's traumas to my own encourages my suspicion that in some way we still live inside 1945, or only a few years after, oozing through a slow-motion version of the Cold War world that followed. As in a Philip K. Dick novel, one which has now become a mediocre television show—yet still, even in that devolved form, has the power to impart its haunting suggestion—*time has stopped*, time itself has been traumatized, and that since midcentury we've been unable to progress beyond the world of that war. After what humankind learned about itself in the first half of the century of Modernity, we're stuck there, doomed to explore its implications forever.

So in a sense I'm *with* Calvino standing on the street watching Mussolini ride past, joined with him there by recollection of my own eight-year-old judgments that Richard Nixon seemed childish *even to a child*, as childish as the cartoon made of him in my parents' leftist newsletters and puppet shows, or in the caricatures of him by Philip Guston and Philip Roth—just as I must now endure explaining to my own children that they're not wrong to judge Donald Trump not only as a bully and a villain but as a *cartoon* of a bully and a villain, one not nearly as compelling or persuasive as Voldemort or Sauron, and to assure them that, no, we weren't wrong to be laughing at him for a year; we were only wrong to believe that we could laugh him away. In the words of Alfred Polgar, "The situation is hopeless but not serious."

In that spirit, a second joke.

This one I heard in a talk by the Slovenian political philosopher Slavoj Žižek, whose writing is full, arguably too full, of jokes. Žižek credits this one to the former German Democratic Republic—the East Germany of the Iron Curtain period, before the fall of the Berlin Wall. I've dovetailed the language, so the joke can dwell in the same universe as the joke from Alphaville (at the risk of repeating myself, this is what novelists do, knit together things not natively joined):

A German worker gets a job in Siberia; aware of how all mail will be read by censors, he tells his friends: "Let's establish a code: if a letter you will get from me is written in ordinary blue ink, it is true; if it is written in red ink, it is false." After a month, his friends get the first letter, written in blue ink: "Everything is wonderful here: stores are full, food is abundant, apartments are large and properly heated, movie theaters show films from the West, there are many beautiful girls ready for an affair—the only thing unavailable is red ink."

Again, the joke plunges us off into the abyss, to fend for ourselves. In Žižek's interpretation, this joke describes the conceptual prison state of what's called "late capitalism"—as consumers in a system that seems on its face to gratify our desires, we nevertheless find certain more indefinable yet essential forms of freedom to be shrinking, yet we lack the very language to protest that life as it is configured. And the channels by which we're allowed to make contact with the greater possibilities of human freedom can seem simultaneously wide-open and strangely diminished—what Bruce Springsteen has called "fifty-seven channels and nothing on." Now, if a reader quickly objects that a Siberian prison camp and late-stage capitalism are two very different things, I'll be the first to agree. Yet in a world defined by an uneasy axis of government and corporate surveillance, it is strangely easy to identify with this concern for the shrinking supply of red ink, even as the joke's aura induces an almost unendurable contemplation of legacies of historical suffering. The joke is full of despair: what can be said without the red ink? Yet what if the joke is *itself* the red ink: that message of ironic resistance which can reach us from within the gulag or corporate prison, those prisons which are everywhere around us?

So, returning to the lessons of "lightness." If my intuitions are correct, then, following Calvino's suggestion, the lightness of art navigates a narrow aperture between *two* realms of unbearable weight—the outer dark of accumulated historical oppressions and inequities—the Gorgon's face of power revealed, forever and again—and the inner burden of *being*, of consciousness itself, the morbidity and inborn sorrow which I found confirmed by the dark memo of my mother's death, and which we find explored with unique capacities by literary artists such as Dostoyevsky and Kafka, or by those who raise humanist philosophical reflection to the level of the literary, such as Kierkegaard, Sartre, and Nietzsche. Ironically, these writers dwell upon precisely the abyssal depths Calvino scarcely ever evokes in his own writing—which is the reason a literary Goth like my teenage self had to wait to embrace Calvino until a bit later.

In Calvino's attempt to characterize art's function, he turns for a comparison to the realm of anthropology: "In response to the precariousness of tribal existence—drought, sickness, and evil forces—a shaman would nullify the weight of his body and fly to another world, another level of perception, where he might find the strength to alter reality." In this, I'm reminded of the memoirist and literary critic Michael Clune, in his essay "Writing against Time": "Defamiliarized perception is supernatural. . . . This is the celebrated experience . . . that science leaves out when it produces descriptions of humans as bundles of automatic processes . . . The virtual work of art is a kind of thinking, a kind of tinkering, a kind of engineering. Its autonomy is that of thought moving in the space between reality and desire."

This, in turn, echoes Calvino's own fascination with the proposals of the pre-Marxist socialist Charles Fourier, whose translated writings Calvino edited and extensively introduced in 1971. Fourier's lovely, preposterous political proposals called for the abolition of school, the family, and marriage in favor of a polymorphous communal society of play-as-work, in which the erotically deprived would be systematically sexually compensated, and children's natural hebephrenic anarchism would be indulged by making them the garbage collectors and waste sorters—speaking of feral children! Fourier's unrealizable vision suggests a pleasure-based utopia analogous to the world of the arts, an antiutilitarian realm that slips the noose of all subsequent drab visions of a merely *economic* utopia, or a merely stable and just social order. They project ahead to such Temporary Autonomous Zones as the Burning Man festival, or the "gift economies" celebrated in Lewis Hyde's *The Gift*.

But I don't really picture Calvino at Burning Man. He was too modest, and he had work to do. The likelihood is that the only lightness Calvino believes attainable is located in the fragile realm of literature, the continuing high-wire act of the linguistic imagination. One final quote from "Lightness": "The word connects the visible trace with the invisible thing, the absent thing, the thing that is desired or feared, like a frail emergency bridge flung over an abyss."

Or, in the words of G.K. Chesterton, "I had found this hole in the world: the fact that one must somehow find a way of loving the world without trusting it."

# In Mugwump Four

I HAD NO INTEREST in Mugwump Four. I was only going to go there to make one point, which was that not everyone and everything that mattered was in there. For instance, Lucinda wasn't. Lucinda had no more interest in Mugwump Four than I did, less. My beloved lived in sublime ignorance of the place. This seemed to me the way to live. Mugwump Four didn't even arouse Lucinda's curiosity, or irritate her, the way it did me. I don't know why it did. The life I lived at this time should have been a sufficiency to me. It was. Only, I felt I had something to contribute, an insight into what had triggered the mad, delusional rush into Mugwump Four by our acquaintances. I wanted to help them. I believed I understood the misapprehension that had inflated the aura of the place, made it appear irresistible. It was not.

Much to the contrary, this was at a time in life when the appeal of such places had diminished to a splendid degree. Lucinda and I had obtained a kind of dream residency, on a hilltop village above Florence, called Fiesole. A small villa there had been bequeathed to our care after the death of the great English poet T_____, as it had been part of T_____'s estate. The great poet had been my mentor, I his protégé. At his death, a decade earlier, I had accepted the duties of literary executor. Inheritance of the villa was the unexpected reward. It carried with it only a provision that the property should be donated back to the conservancy of the town of Fiesole, rather than sold, when we had exhausted its usefulness.

The villa was a well-preserved seventeenth-century stone construction, naturally self-cooling, managed by the nearest neighbors, a family of tradespeople who'd lived in their own more modest house for five or six generations. They had adored T_____ and now cared for us as a natural extension of that love. It sat high above the village, much as the village sat above the panorama of steep, winding roads down into the valleys and back into Florence itself. With only a brief walk to a spring to refill our plastic liter bottles, and a slightly longer walk into the village to the market, there were many days when we never started the car. The village had a tiny number of restaurants and a small hotel, but for the most part it entertained only day tourists, who bused up from Florence for a glimpse of the ruins. We avoided them easily and heard barely any English spoken except by ourselves.

Each day we sat out on the terrace, in the sweet breezes that made the Italian afternoons tolerable, drinking coffee, working on our laptops. Lucinda was finishing her third novel. I knew it would be her best. I labored at my philosophical treatise, *Another Realm Yet*, into which I had poured the effort of a lifetime. Though it might be discursive, it also reflected my training in aesthetics begun under T_____, and I planned to dedicate it to him, as tribute and thanks. Our only visitors in this time were the cats who daily slid between our feet petitioning for food. We kept a supply of single-portion cans of cat food which we'd pry open and set out in the shade.

I hesitate to call these cats feral, since the word suggests a kind of wariness or ferocity that wasn't the case. Rather, these cats were collectively domesticated to the town of Fiesole, surely through many generations. They belonged to the villa, and the villa to them, perhaps more than Lucinda and myself. We loved them. That season, before I began my wanderings in Mugwump Four, there was one we especially loved. A cat so yellow it was nearly lemon-colored, it was the boldest in seeking affection, and would flop onto the stones of the terrace and allow Lucinda to stroke the fur of its throat and stomach while it purred and arched. Quite marvelously, this yellow cat was accompanied on its visits by a small tortoise, who would invariably inch from the rock garden onto our terrace and sun itself while the cat fed. More than once we saw the yellow cat, in her ecstasies of contact, rub her cheek against the ridge of the tortoise's shell. They seemed to be the best of friends.

Why should Mugwump Four trouble me so? I couldn't answer this question. The success of the place seemed an insult. It was either relevant or irrelevant to my life's researches, but I couldn't decide which. Lucinda would laugh when she glanced at my laptop and saw that I was dabbling around its edges.

"You're wasting time," she said. "You'll never understand it doing that. Take the plunge, if you're so curious. It won't kill you."

"What do you know about it?"

"It didn't kill me. I went and came back."

I felt disconcerted. "I didn't realize you'd ever gone there."

"Three years ago, when we were apart."

"Ah." I stood, went through the French doors to the kitchen, and made myself another cappuccino, frothing the foam, shaking on just a dash of cocoa. I didn't speak again until Lucinda's attention had returned to her screen, so she had to look up when I did. Was this passive-aggressive on my part? "It's just that I didn't think of it as something you'd care for."

"Mugwump Four isn't all one thing," she said. "There were parts I cared for, parts I didn't. I can't explain it to you."

"I'm sure you could if you liked. But the point is, you stopped. Most people don't."

She shrugged. "I don't have an addictive personality. Maybe even the reverse."

"You never think of going back?"

She spread her hands and smiled, as if to say: Why would I choose to be anywhere but here?


The confidence that came so easily to Lucinda was for me unattainable. Never mind the assertion, possibly chimerical, that one could possess "an addictive personality," or its reverse. I was sure it was Lucinda's ebullience, that joy in the simple pleasures of daily life, which bloomed so easily in her, which had protected her from the snares and labyrinths of Mugwump Four. I'd never known her to be either enthralled or perplexed by illusions. Lucinda tended, instead, to dismiss them. She was subtle, and watchful, but never morbid. I loved her for it.

I knew too well my own argumentative compulsions. I believed I had something to say to the souls who'd given themselves to Mugwump Four, if, once inside, I could make them listen. In light of this, I should remain humble and take every precaution against becoming obsessed.

I had a triple plan, which I shared with Lucinda.

"Write down a question only you would be able to answer," I told her. "The prompt for a secret only you know. Don't include the answer, and don't let me see it. Fold it into a small square, and tape it to the back of my desk drawer." Though we worked most mornings on the terrace, I had with Lucinda's blessings laid claim to T_____'s magnificent old scarred oaken desk, a kind of talismanic object for me.

"I don't have any secrets from you."

"Something inconsequential. A detail from childhood that you've never told anyone."

I added a note to myself, a piece of nonsense I'd never written down or mentioned aloud, a pun which had always itched my mind: "Spanielkopita." I folded it and taped it in that same place, on the back panel of the upper drawer of my desk. Should I become confused in Mugwump Four, as I'd learned was possible, I could look there. The mere evidence of the presence of the notes would make the first test. The nonsense note to myself, a second. The third, Lucinda's secret, would insulate me from the risk being beguiled by some simulacrum of her—a projection derived from the evidence of my own senses.

"Then you're going in, at last?"

"Yes."

"You're like a knight on a quest. Or an astronaut stepping into the void."

"Don't mock me. Yes."

"I am your tether."

"Always."


My virtual house was negligible, generic. I didn't work on it at all. I wasn't seeking to lure others into some narcissistic exoskeletal avatar decorated with my loves and hates, my trophies and souvenirs. Least of all would I drag any representation of Lucinda into this space, brandishing her as if a trinket. It seemed a kind of violence, though so many apparently disagreed. Let my domicile here be cut-and-paste, to mark my indifference. The sky above my house was the color of a "404 page not found" error message.

I sought instead the town square, the crossroads. Let me be the Diogenes or Bartleby of Mugwump Four, to confront them with the essential barrenness of its delights. I put out a shingle with my first offering, for anyone who cared to notice. It was an essay I'd written, titled "A View Needs a Frame." An essay, or, in the local parlance, a "broadside."

From the first I was mesmerized. The wonders of nature were here, presented with such fulsomeness and ingenuity and velocity. No traveler could ever have known them all. Children and animals of all species cavorted in wondrous variety. Some of their tricks I could watch on repeat for what felt like hours. To be in this place was to be in the vortex of the human catastrophe: the appetite for attention and the rage for fame, the terror of boredom, the yearning for some spiritual contemplative stillness forever aroused and then snuffed out in a panic at what it might uncover. I knew this from my research, my peerings-in from the exterior. Yet to occupy this place from within was to feel it as one feels one's own body.

This was true from the very first encounter in which I involved myself. A young man with a Rasputin beard and gentle eyes stopped and considered my broadside's headline. "A view needs a frame?"

"Yes!" I said. "I wrote it to show that despite our fascination with infinite possibility, we really yearn to have an aesthetic selection made on our behalf, by another human sensibility of some kind. It's in the relation between the limit and the expanse, the momentary and the eternal, the individual and collective experience, that meaning is generated—"

"Orgasm!" he cried.

"What?"

"I Orgasmed your broadside."

"But you haven't read the essay."

"Don't need to! Get it already. Have you tried bathing with a hippopotamus?"

"I'm sorry?"

"Look. Here's a frame, just like you were saying. Look no further. I'm the 'sensibility of some kind.'" He unfolded a door in the air. Through it I glimpsed an amusing scene, done in black and white, a rotogravure depicting a man in a Victorian-style moustache swimming peacefully along the back of the animal in question, which carried on its face a benign smile almost of the Mona Lisa variety. The man's clothes were heaped on a low brick wall at the water's edge. The hippo snorted two tiny pillars of water from its nostrils, like miniature whale spouts. Beneath, in antique newsprint font, were the words "Bathing with a Hippopotamus."

"People tend to dig it," said the bearded man. He held the door open, invitingly. It seemed harmless enough. I went inside.

The water was a fine temperature, and the hide of the animal pleasingly velvety and smooth. The image was still rendered in black and white, with minute crosshatching to form the illusion of volume; this included my own arms now where they clutched the hippo's soft shoulder. Yet I felt the creature breathing under my touch. It rolled, gently, in the waves, then immersed, to breathe underwater. With gladness I descended too, and we blew bubbles there together before returning to the surface.

What number of minutes or hours I spent there, in an effervescent joy beside this creature, I can't know. At one point the sequence appeared to glitch, then return to its starting point, yet in my ecstasy I felt concerned less to examine the seams of the confabulation than to replenish my spirit within its artistry, so absurd and sublime at once.

One day—for now it began to feel that weeks had passed—I noticed that while our sky remained dotted only with the mildest of passing clouds, the walls of our bathing chamber, if one dove deep enough, were dotted with underwater porticos. These made entrances to stone caves. Indeed, light seemed to emanate from the mouths of these caves, and when one swam nearer—as I did now—one discovered bright neon-colored salutations and exhortations. These headlines were the first color I had seen since entering the rotogravure world.

*IF YOU LIKE BATHING WITH A HIPPOPOTAMUS YOU'LL GO BERSERK FOR JET-SKIING WITH A PTERODACTYL*

*CONSIDER AN UPGRADE TO BATHOPOTAMUS.2 NOW WITH ABSTRACT RECURSION AND INTRINSIC ELUCIDATION*

*CALL YOUR MOTHER*

Each of these brought me ever-so-slightly back to myself, but it was when I swam further and saw TOP FIVE REASONS TO RECONSIDER BATHING WITH A HIPPOPOTAMUS that I reconstituted my purpose here. This was the temper of conversation I should seek: the skeptics and cautionaries within Mugwump Four, those who might be amenable to my arguments. I swam down into the cave entrance lit by this banner.

"Step this way." It was a young child, a girl, with the ears of a mouse. I obeyed. We descended a circular stair. I saw that I was now wearing a jumpsuit, like some garage mechanic. Yet immaculate as the robes of a saint. The mouse-girl, when I looked up again, wore them as well. She'd grown taller, as tall as me. Her whole face had become that of a mouse, and now she was without gender, though I felt some residue of "girl" and "child" hung about her.

"What are the top five reasons?" I asked her.

"Number one: It is highly dangerous to bathe near a hippopotamus." This was intoned as if by the voice of some ancient sage or wizard. "More people are killed each year by hippopotamuses than by vending machines."

"Wait, that can't be what you mean to say."

"I have the statistics right here," said the tall mouse.

"No, I mean on the level of rhetoric. No one fears vending machines. In making your comparison you should contrast the apparently benign hippo with something that generates irrational and disproportionate fear, like an apex predator—a lion or shark, say."

"A vending machine is a kind of predator."

"You may have something there," I admitted. "At least, I admire the cast of mind that would suggest such a thing."

"Thank you. For reasons two through four, please upgrade to Mugwump Five."

"Mugwump Five? I've only begun adjusting to Mugwump Four." This was overstatement if anything was. I'd seen so little of the place. "Adjustment" seemed inconceivable.

"You only need to take my hand," said the tall mouse.

"Thank you," I said. I worked to repossess my sense of purpose. "I cherish the offer. I just need to prepare . . ."

"Of course. You'll want to take a moment inform your acolytes when you migrate, so they can locate you there in the new place. In Mugwump Five."

"My acolytes? Oh, yes." At this I noticed the various digits arrayed in peripheral vision. I still had only "Zero" acolytes—perhaps this statistic was invisible to the tall mouse?—but my "*view needs a frame*" broadside had been Orgasmed 3,567 times.

"I've got work to do," I told the mouse, who, I noticed now, had a tiny bird perched on the left shoulder of its robes. A canary, black and yellow. The canary groomed fondly at the mouse's ear, then nudged the crown of its tiny head into the mouse's whiskers. "I'm working on a new broadside," I told the mouse and the canary. "The subject is how this era of virtuality and mediation leaves us all starved for the essential somatic life—that's to say, for the pleasures of the body, of proximity and locality. For simply being with another creature, bathed in affection and wonder." At that moment I noticed that a small green mantis crawled on the yellow feathers of the canary's shoulder and nudged its wide-eyed, triangular head against one corner of the canary's beak. "This accounts for the extraordinary profusion of video clips of various animals snuggling with humans, and with other species different from their own. The current craze for bathing with hippopotamuses, or should it be hippopotami, for instance—" Further examples were near to hand, but I left this to implication. "The more the protocols and subroutines plunge us into an abyss of estrangement, the more we sentimentalize even the most rudimentary gestures of connection and recognition. Utterances like 'Laugh Out Loud!' or the 'awwwwwww,' which invariably accompanies evocations of cute animals or babies, are like the decanted residual expressions of the bodies we can no longer locate in real space. I should be writing all this down."

"Perhaps it's just you," said the canary, though I thought I'd addressed the mouse. "Many people thrill to images of glistening machines fucking and fighting in an abstracted rendering that completely eschews the texture of the 'natural' or 'real.' Have a look, for instance, at Celebrity Rave Exo-Skins, or Orb Void Spandex."

I shuddered. "It's a version of the Stockholm syndrome," I suggested. "Siding with the captor, making a total identification with the antihuman domain."

"We've got it all on offer," said the mantis, as if in perfect agreement.

"No, but that's just the point. The whole world *isn't* here in Mugwump Four; it just feels that way while you're immersed. Not everything has been digitized, not even a small percentage, really. Vast realms of human history and culture are completely unrepresented here! We don't feel what we're missing at the conscious level, but the sacrifice is tragic. We've denied ourselves, too, the company of those who can't afford Mugwump Four, or have been disinclined to try it, or have never even heard of it—we've partitioned ourselves from much of our commonality with our human species. Until quite recently I was on the other side of that partition myself."

"Well, thank Christ, then, that you've made it here at last," said a tardigrade perched on the lower rim of the mantis's ear. The tardigrade, that nearly subatomically tiny creature who could

survive at the bottom of the ocean and in the deep void of space—
I had to admit that it was truly miraculous that it was visible to my
naked eye—had a most endearingly small conical snout, which it
nuzzled against the mantis's ear-rim.

"You believe in Christ?" Even as I formed this question, I
found myself distracted by the bright throbbing fire of the numeral 1 at my peripheral vision. I glanced to see what it signified.
I had gained an acolyte—my first! (The number of Orgasms my
first broadside collected continued to rocket into the hundreds of
thousands now, the digit counter a racing blur. I had to admit it
really was a popular broadside.)

"Ah, just a moment," I said to the tardigrade, the mantis, the
canary, and the mouse. Insatiably curious, I clicked on my acolyte's moniker, HippoBathLover77.

HippoBathLover77 was a silverback gorilla, unmistakably
masculine. "There you are," he said, in a tone of grim relief, as if
he'd been waiting for some time.

"Sorry."

He waved me off, then led me down a corridor, to a low doorway. "Frame," he said. "Get it? Don't bump your head."

"I appreciate the reference," I said.

"Great broadside, dude."

"Thank you."

The domicile was dark and small. Inside, I met the gorilla's
companion animal, as I should by now have expected. It was a capybara, the world's largest rodent. The gorilla caught me staring. "We
mammals got to stick together," he said. As on cue, the capybara

nudged its head into the gorilla's thigh. The gorilla scratched behind its ear. "All that bird-reptile-insect interspecies stuff? For me, that's just going a bit too far. Makes me queasy, to be honest."

"I know what you mean," I said, wanting to placate him.

"Welcome to the Vale of the Diagnosticians," said the gorilla. "Which is pretty much just me and this guy." He patted the capybara's head. "The vast majority in here aren't capable of the least bit of critical perspective."

"That's true in so many cases."

We feel your critiques are right on target," said the gorilla. "In fact, you probably don't even grasp the extent of it."

"Oh, I believe I do."

"Look around you, take it in, because it won't be here much longer. Mugwump Four is collapsing."

"Really?" This wasn't what I'd expected to hear. "Collapsing? Are you sure?"

"Oh, sure. Totally unsustainable. The sheeple just don't know it yet. Like Yogi Berra said, nobody comes here anymore, it's too crowded. I'm surprised you bothered."

"I thought it was my responsibility to say something. Nearly everyone I know is inside this place, to my dismay."

"Forget it, don't waste your time. They'll never pay any attention."

"Well, if my first broadside is any example . . ." I didn't want to appear immodest. "It would seem that many here are starved for an interrogation of this so-called experience, one coming from within."

"Don't kid yourself. Check your click-through."

The gorilla had a point. The Orgasms were now in the seven figures, yet when I delved into my statistics, to discover how many had actually viewed the broadside, the number turned out to be seventeen. Worse, the numbers indicated that only five had read it to the end. I'd attracted two comments. From FRAMESAREFORFASCISTS21, "Sit on a xylophone!" From HippoBathLover77, "Call me." Apparently, passersby had garlanded the thing with Orgasms indifferently, as a reflex. It was possible they'd never even read to the end of the broadside's title.

It now occurred to me to ask, "Why did you pick that particular name—HippoBathLover?"

"Eh, that was a long time ago. Just never got around to changing it."

"Well, this was just my first broadside," I said. "I've got a great deal to say."

Now the capybara spoke. "Talk to him about reification."

"Oh, yeah," said the gorilla. "There's that, too."

"Reification? In what sense?"

"You're like me, right? You want to see this place fold up under the pressure its own contradictions, the sooner the better."

"Absolutely," I said. "This is a terrible place. I mean, it's not just that each thing simply follows the last with no sense of proportion or congruence. But the texture, the rendering—it's all so thin, so paltry, so underfurnished. How preposterous that anyone could mistake it for an entire world!"

"Now, hold your horses," said the gorilla, sounding defensive. "You get into it what you put out. You're new. Frankly, you didn't put a whole lot of effort into curation."

"I was eager to enter the fray."

"Yeah, well, that leads me to the other thing."

"Reification," reminded the capybara.

"Exactly," agreed the gorilla. "The more you cobble up these essays of yours, critiquing Mugwump Four from within, the more real you make it. Reinvigoration, reinscription, reification—it's a mug's game. Every minute of human attention invested in contemplating the nature of this horseshit scenario, even pointing out its faults or instabilities—the greater the attentional investment. Yours and your reader's."

"I hadn't considered."

"That's why it's lucky we found you."

"What do you advise instead?"

"Scram, vamoose, get out now, while the getting's good. Go for the upgrade. Mugwump Five is where it's at."

"I don't want the upgrade—"

"All you have to do is high-five the capybara. Pun intended!" Indeed, the capybara had now raised its coarse-haired paw as if in mournful salute. "The rest takes care of itself. Contrary to any rumors going around, your acolytes will transfer instantly—"

"No, thank you. My preference is for creating avenues back out. Portals to the real world."

"Listen, that's admirable. We all hold the real world in highest regard around here. It's the inspiration for everything we do."

I struggled to contain my impatience with this argument, which had begun to seem little more than a sales pitch. "More than inspiration, I'd think. Consider the energy required to cool the servers. One shouldn't forget that this etheric realm is supported by a vast armature of groaning machines, occupying a terribly literal footprint in a hidden desert quadrant of Utah, guarded by razor wire and armed guards. Just because all this is kept out of sight doesn't mean it shouldn't remain in our thoughts."

"It's not out of sight in Mugwump Five. You can break in through subterranean tunnels and explore the whole fortress from the inside, fight the guards, destroy the machine with your bare hands, liberate the slaves. It's a hugely popular feature!"

"You mean some kind of gamified virtual rendering of the actual server farm? That's perverse."

The gorilla shrugged. "Many things are."

A numeral 2 pulsed, just then, on the horizon. An acolyte. *LightAsATether1*.

"Will you excuse me?"

"High-five him!" urged the gorilla. The capybara widened its eyes, which were rimmed, I thought, with tears.

"In a moment, I promise."

Lucinda placed a warm cup in my hands where I sat, blinking in the morning light, on the terrace. The coffee, the foam atop the coffee, the faint rime of cocoa along the foam, all were perfect. It was an exemplary instance of the exquisite care Lucinda took. The care she took over *me*, her replenishing capacity for anticipating my needs before I'd expressed them. Had I been slumbering here in my chair? When had I last told her I loved her? The sunlight, filtering through haze, was gorgeous and indeterminate.

"Was there an animal here? Just now?"

"Only the yellow cat," she said. "It went under your chair, a minute ago."

"We should feed it."

"I'll put out a can," she said, and turned inside.

I sat and felt the sun begin to warm my body and the stones of the terrace beneath my bare feet. I wore my robe, as if I'd indeed been asleep.

"You brought me back," I said wonderingly, when Lucinda returned to place the open tin of cat food on the stones.

She only smiled.

"You knew how to find me."

"You weren't so hard to find," she said. "I only needed to reach out my hand."

"You truly are my tether. I cherish you." Then, struck, as if possessed, I put aside my coffee and dashed in through the French doors, to my desk. To T_____'s desk. Such a beautiful, substantive thing, steeped in time, vehicle for such awesome accumulations of meaning, from the trees which had been chopped down to build it and the craft of those who'd fitted the wood, to my mentor's poems, his copious masterworks, which had been written there, in fountain pen, in a series of blue notebooks. My own modest efforts, too, my unfinished treatise, stacked there in the recentest draft.

Lucinda stood in the doorway, watching.

I pulled out the drawer. The two folded slips of paper remained taped at the back. I shouldn't have doubted I'd see them there.

"A riddle, my love!"

"Yes?" she asked.

"One of my own invention: What do you call a phyllo dough pastry that is capable of fetching sticks?"

"I can't guess," she said. "What is it?"

I freed my own slip of paper, that one on which I'd scribbled my foolish pun, from the drawer back, and thrust it into her hands. "Read it!"

Lucinda unfolded it, smiled again. It was too much to expect her to laugh.

"Now your secret," I said. I loosened the second slip from the drawer. "May I read it?"

"That's up to you."

"Do you remember what you wrote?"

"I remember."

"I'll test you on it."

"Don't be silly," she said. "How could I fail? Only be certain, my love. One doesn't always wish to know a secret."

"I do."

"Fair enough. Only—come outside."

The sun had parted the haze. The morning glistened. The yellow cat and its turtle friend fed, heads nudged and bobbing together, from the tin of cat food. I unfolded Lucinda's slip of paper. It read, *AREN'T YOU PLEASED WITH THE UPGRADE?*

# Secret Bibliography

*An incomplete concordance of* termite operations, *partially ac-knowledged artifacts, gift-economy gestures, and so on.*

1976–77, *Fig Leaf Man* comics, cocreator/writer (with Jim Feast), seven issues.

1987/88, *Idiot Tooth Magazine,* coeditor/publisher (with Shelley Jackson), two issues.

1989–98, *Dream World News*, cofounder (with Luke Jaeger and Shoshana Marchand) and contributing editor.

2000, *The Best of Crank*, anthology, editor Bryan Cholfin. Three uncollected short stories. Tor Books.

2006, (with photographer Kate Milford) *Patchwork Planet*, photographs and essays on downtown Brooklyn. BookCourt/Soft Skull.

2006, coauthor (as "Harris Conklin"), with Christopher Sorrentino ("Ivan Felt"), *Believeniks: The Year We Wrote a Book about the Mets*, Doubleday.

2007– ongoing, *The Promiscuous Materials Project*, online collaboration generator, Internet.

2007–8, (with Karl Rusnak, Farel Dalrymple, Gary Panter, Paul Hornschemeier), *Omega the Unknown*, comic book, ten issues, Marvel Comics.

2008, (with Walter Salas-Humara and The Elegant Two), as "I'm Not Jim," *You Are All My People*, album, Bloodshot Records.

2009, "Chaldron Glasses," (artifact), *The Thing Quarterly,* Jonn Herschend and Will Rogan, curators, issue 7.

2014, *Friday at Enrico's* (completion of unfinished novel by Don Carpenter), Counterpoint Press.

2016, (with Laurence Rickels), *The Blot: A Supplement*, Anti-Oedipus Press.

2017– ongoing (as "Jojo," with Samuel Sousa), *Radio Free Aftermath* radio show, KSPC 88.7 FM.

2022, *Horse with No Cake: Selected Poems and Lyrics*, Another Sun Press.

# About the Author

HTTPS://JONATHANLETHEM.COM

# FRIENDS OF

These are indisputably momentous times— the financial system is melting down globally and the Empire is stumbling. Now more than ever there is a vital need for radical ideas.

In the years since its founding—and on a mere shoestring—PM Press has risen to the formidable challenge of publishing and distributing knowledge and entertainment for the struggles ahead. With hundreds of releases to date, we have published an impressive and stimulating array of literature, art, music, politics, and culture. Using every available medium, we've succeeded in connecting those hungry for ideas and information to those putting them into practice.

Friends of PM allows you to directly help impact, amplify, and revitalize the discourse and actions of radical writers, filmmakers, and artists. It provides us with a stable foundation from which we can build upon our early successes and provides a much-needed subsidy for the materials that can't necessarily pay their own way. You can help make that happen—and receive every new title automatically delivered to your door once a month—by joining as a Friend of PM Press. And, we'll throw in a free T-shirt when you sign up.

Here are your options:
- $30 a month: Get all books and pamphlets plus 50% discount on all webstore purchases
- $40 a month: Get all PM Press releases (including CDs and DVDs) plus 50% discount on all webstore purchases
- $100 a month: Superstar—Everything plus PM merchandise, free downloads, and 50% discount on all webstore purchases

For those who can't afford $30 or more a month, we have Sustainer Rates at $15, $10, and $5. Sustainers get a free PM Press T-shirt and a 50% discount on all purchases from our website.

Your Visa or Mastercard will be billed once a month, until you tell us to stop. Or until our efforts succeed in bringing the revolution around. Or the financial meltdown of Capital makes plastic redundant. Whichever comes first.

PM Press is an independent, radical publisher of critically necessary books for our tumultuous times. Our aim is to deliver bold political ideas and vital stories to all walks of life and arm the dreamers to demand the impossible. Founded in 2007 by a small group of people with decades of publishing, media, and organizing experience, we have sold millions of copies of our books, most often one at a time, face to face. We're old enough to know what we're doing and young enough to know what's at stake. Join us to create a better world.

PM Press
PO Box 23912
Oakland, CA 94623
info@pmpress.org

PM Press in Europe
europe@pmpress.org
www.pmpress.org.uk

PM PRESS OUTSPOKEN AUTHORS

**JOHN CROWLEY**
TOTALITOPIA
*Plus...*

"... a genius with the imagination for ten ordinary writers."
—URSULA K. LE GUIN

PM PRESS OUTSPOKEN AUTHORS

**SAMUEL R. DELANY**
THE ATHEIST IN
THE ATTIC
*Plus...*

"A talent very close to time travel—or magic."
—LOCUS

PM PRESS OUTSPOKEN AUTHORS

**MICHAEL BLUMLEIN**
THOREAU'S MICROSCOPE
*Plus...*

"Blumlein has an exceptional vision, and he conveys it with exceptional talent."
—WASHINGTON POST

PM PRESS OUTSPOKEN AUTHORS

**RACHEL POLLACK**
THE BEATRIX GATES
*Plus...*

"Here be magick . . . A fully matured creative consciousness!"
—GREAT PLAINS LITERATURE OF IDAS

PM PRESS OUTSPOKEN AUTHORS

**PAUL PARK**
A CITY MADE OF WORDS
*Plus...*

"A brilliant, stunning, frightening, major, major talent."
—GENE WOLFE

PM PRESS OUTSPOKEN AUTHORS

**NISI SHAWL**
TALK LIKE A MAN
*Plus...*

"Nisi is brilliant."
—AMAL EL-MOHTAR

PM PRESS OUTSPOKEN AUTHORS

**MEG ELISON**
BIG GIRL
*Plus...*

"Compelling and fierce and unstoppable."
—PAT MURPHY, WORLD FANTASY AWARD WINNER

PM PRESS OUTSPOKEN AUTHORS

**NICK MAMATAS**
THE PLANETBREAKER'S SON
*Plus...*

"One of the most inventive, fascinating, and distinctive voices in the field."
—LOCUS MAGAZINE

PM PRESS OUTSPOKEN AUTHORS

**VANDANA SINGH**
UTOPIAS OF THE THIRD KIND
*Plus...*

"She's the most original and mythical voices in recent SF."
—JEAN A. WOLF, LOCUS

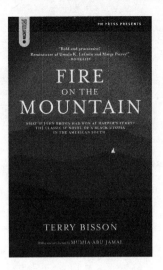

## Fire on the Mountain

**Terry Bisson**

**Introduction by Mumia Abu-Jamal**

ISBN: 978-1-60486-087-0

208 pages • 5 x 8 • $18.95

It's 1959 in socialist Virginia. The Deep South is an independent Black nation called Nova Africa. The second Mars expedition is about to touch down on the red planet. And a pregnant scientist is climbing the Blue Ridge in search of her great-great grandfather, a teenage slave who fought with John Brown and Harriet Tubman's guerrilla army.

Long unavailable in the U.S., published in France as *Nova Africa*, *Fire on the Mountain* is the story of what might have happened if John Brown's raid on Harper's Ferry had succeeded—and the Civil War had been started not by the slave owners but the abolitionists.

> *"History revisioned, turned inside out . . . Bisson's*
> *wild and wonderful imagination has taken some*
> *strange turns to arrive at such a destination."*
> —Madison Smartt Bell, Anisfield-Wolf Award
> winner and author of *Devil's Dream*

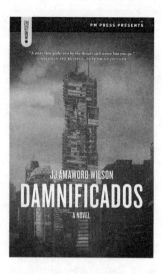

## Damnificados

**JJ Amaworo Wilson**

ISBN: 978-1-62963-117-2

288 pages • 5 x 8 • $15.95

*Damnificados* is loosely based on the real-life occupation of a half-completed skyscraper in Caracas, Venezuela, the Tower of David. In this fictional version, six hundred "damnificados"—vagabonds and misfits—take over an abandoned urban tower and set up a community complete with schools, stores, beauty salons, bakeries, and a rag-tag defensive militia. Their always heroic (and often hilarious) struggle for survival and dignity pits them against corrupt police, the brutal military, and the tyrannical "owners."

Taking place in an unnamed country at an unspecified time, the novel has elements of magical realism: avenging wolves, biblical floods, massacres involving multilingual ghosts, arrow showers falling to the tune of Beethoven's Ninth, and a trash truck acting as a Trojan horse. The ghosts and miracles woven into the narrative are part of a richly imagined world in which the laws of nature are constantly stretched and the past is always present.

> *"Should be read by every politician and rich bastard and then force-fed to them—literally, page by page."*
> —Jimmy Santiago Baca, author of *A Place to Stand*